Watching the Sparks Fly

"We have a great basketball team," Franny tells Victory. "You play?"

Victory shakes her head and makes a face.

"I'm opposed to anything where you wear a uniform. Plus . . . basketball is for preppy types who are trying to get extracurricular stuff so they can get into Brown or Yale."

Franny says quietly, "I'm captain of the team." She pauses. "Too bad you feel that way. We could use someone like you. Someone . . . hefty."

Victory stares right at Franny, smiles and says, "Well . . . I'd love to stay and chat but I only have one minute." And she sticks up her middle finger at Franny to indicate the number one!

"Well," I say, trying to be peacemaker, "you can be anything you want at Barrow. There's room for everybody."

But Franny just stands there. And so does Victory.

After a second, Franny speaks. "Right," she says. "Whatever you do at Barrow's okay . . . within the bounds of good taste."

Uh oh.

Victory picks right up on that one. "Good taste? What's that?"

Franny responds calmly. "Maybe you'll find out."

I don't think Franny and Victory and I are going to be best friends.

Maybe I'll Move To The Lost & Found

Susan Haven

AN ARCHWAY PAPERBACK
Published by POCKET BOOKS
New York   London   Toronto   Sydney   Tokyo

An Archway Paperback published by
POCKET BOOKS, a division of Simon & Schuster Inc.
1230 Avenue of the Americas, New York, NY 10020

Copyright © 1988 by Susan Haven
Cover art copyright © 1989 Carl Cassler

Published by arrangement with G. P. Putnam's Sons
Library of Congress Catalog Card Number: 87-24942

ISBN: 0-671-67402-1

First Archway Paperback printing March 1989

10 9 8 7 6 5 4 3 2

AN ARCHWAY PAPERBACK and colophon are
registered trademarks of Simon & Schuster Inc.

Printed in the U.S.A.

IL 7+

To Paul and Paula
with love and thanks

Chapter 1

I'm sitting on my hallway floor because I'm locked out of my apartment again. I stick my hand into my pocketbook one last time. Pretzel salt but no keys.

I forget my keys a lot. I forget a lot of things . . . a lot. When I graduate from the Barrow School they'll probably rename the Lost and Found "The Gilly Miles Memorial Foundation." I go there every day just in case. Only this afternoon I found one of my Afghanistani woven mittens. Too bad it's almost spring.

I hope I didn't lose my keys in the Lost and Found. If I did, I swear, I'm going to give myself up for adoption. I can't stand myself sometimes.

My mom says I shouldn't talk that way. My dad says, "If you don't like yourself, Gilly, who will?" They're right, of course. A kid should like herself. Be proud of herself. Be glad she's she. And I'm not.

1

I hate that about myself.

It's four o'clock. My mom is working today and won't be home till six. Franny Hodges, my best friend and next-door neighbor, is still at Barrow for basketball practice and won't be home till five. And Mrs. Hearn in 11C, right opposite my apartment, has moved into a senior citizens' hotel. She was always home. We'd sit and have milk and cookies, and talk about how forgetful we both were. Now her apartment is empty.

I tried doing my homework, I really did. I opened my *Julius Caesar* book. But I closed it. A person can get seriously ill if she tries to do the day's homework too soon after the day is over.

The elevator. I hear the elevator rumbling to a stop.

The heavy metal door slides open, and Franny Hodges walks out.

"Gilly . . . not again!"

"Yes, again!" I reply defensively. "I'm going for *The Guinness Book of Records*."

Franny laughs as she takes off her hat and shakes her wool-flattened hair. Miraculously, her soft blond curls return to their usual fluffy and perfect places.

Franny happens to be very pretty. Okay, she's actually beautiful.

I have curls too—brown ones—but when my hat flattens and uglies them, they stay flat and ugly.

I get up silently, watch as Franny unlocks her door, and follow her into 11B. When we reach her bedroom, I drop my books, my bag, and my bod onto her bed.

"Tough day?" says Franny.

I nod. "Well, it was actually good and bad. My father

2

called. My brother, Jeff, is getting this big science award at his high school tomorrow night and we all have to show up. Me with Mom. Dad with Airhead."

Airhead is my dad's girlfriend. Her name's really Abigail but I call her Airhead because she does soap commercials on TV and because her brain would float on water.

"And what's the good news?"

"The good news is that it isn't tomorrow night yet. I'm terrified. I haven't seen my father in a month."

"Well, then, don't go."

"My brother would be really hurt. I have to."

Franny nods. "You're a good person, Gilly Miles."

I smile. Franny is beautiful, bright, stylish, and vice president of our class. I'd hate her guts but she is also so so nice. She even got Robert Jason, the school president, to appoint me Class Sergeant at Arms. What an embarrassing job. What am I supposed to do? Stand by the door and keep out terrorists?

I'll be honest. I want to do more than just be sergeant at arms. I want to accomplish something, make a contribution, be outstanding. I want to be a leader too.

Of course, being relatively shy, I just don't want anybody to notice.

"Well, I had a lousy day too," Franny continues. "They canceled basketball practice. Would you believe Barrow rented the gym again?"

Barrow, our private school, is always short of money, so they rent out the facilities.

"That's a shame," I say.

To tell you the truth, I don't care that much about

girls' basketball. I know missing practice upsets Franny, but this is her biggest problem in life. That and if her VCR breaks and she can't tape her favorite soap operas. She even has two parents who've been married twenty years and still love each other.

She sighs. "Let's play 'Who Shall I Marry?' It'll cheer us both up, okay?"

"Great idea."

She opens her pink night-table drawer and takes out a deck of cards.

"O great cards," she chants as she pulls out the four aces, "O great seers of tomorrow, predictors of our fate, we ask you today who Gillian Miles, my best and dearest and oldest friend, will marry. Who will fill her life with love, with passion, and with sex. We seek the answer, cards, in your wise predictions. . . . Tell us, O cards . . . tell us—"

"All right already, Fran! By the time the cards tell me who I'm going to marry, I'll be too old to bear children."

"Sorry. I got carried away."

"Anyway, I don't want to play it today. You do it."

"Me?" She hesitates one millisecond. "Well . . . all right."

She hands me the cards and I lay the four aces on the bedspread. Each ace stands for a boy you might marry.

"Okay . . . I assume your first ace is Don Melnick."

Franny nods. Don Melnick is president of the senior high school class and has a crush on Franny.

"Next is Bill Levy."

Bill Levy is captain of the ninth-grade softball team and also has a crush on Franny.

4

"Mr. Morani."

Mr. Morani is the gym teacher—and it is altogether possible that he also may have a crush on Franny.

"And, finally"—Franny points to the ace of spades—"Master X."

"Master X. Again? Who is he?"

Franny looks at me. "I can't say. All I can tell you is that he doesn't go to our school. And he's gorgeous and smart and talented and sensitive and has the cutest behind on the West Side of New York."

I know who she's talking about, but I pretend I don't.

"Franny, I'm your best friend. You can tell me. We tell each other everything."

"I just can't. Not yet. What if we have a fight? What if it gets back to Ronnie or Toby? I'd die. I just can't trust you yet. Don't take it personally."

I nod. I pretend to be hurt.

"Okay," I start. "What do you want to know?"

The way this game works is that first you ask the cards a question, and then you deal out cards one at a time across the four aces. When a card from the deck lands on the same suit as one of the aces, that guy is the answer to your question.

"Okay," Franny begins, "which of these guys is thinking about me right this very second?"

I begin to deal. On the fifth card I turn up a heart, which lands on the ace of hearts. Don Melnick.

"Great," Franny says. "Okay, who will ask me out to the auction party?"

Barrow has a big auction to raise money, and the kids

5

have a dance afterwards. Barrow has more fund-raising events than educational TV.

I deal. This time the match is Master X!

Franny's entire face lights up like a G.E. "soft light" bulb.

"Grreat! Greeeat! I'm going to make that happen, I really am! This is so great, I can't believe it!"

Anything can make Franny happy because she's happy to begin with. I wish I were more like her. I wish I had her style. Her outgoing personality. Her looks. Her optimism. Her belt collection.

Suddenly the doorbell rings.

"Could you get that, Gil?"

"Sure." I get up and go to the door. Maybe it's my prince. Maybe it's my fairy godmother. Maybe it's the President begging me to overcome my shyness and be his personal adviser on teenage problems. Maybe it's my mother with the key.

I open the door.

Unfortunately, it's none of the above. It's only reality. It's the one person who's crazy about me. It's my upstairs neighbor, Arnold Dorfenberg, son of the sixth-floor Dorfenbergs, Norman and Selma.

Chapter 2

*A*rnold *pushes his glasses back up his nose with his* index finger and clears his throat.

"I thought you'd be here, Gil," he says. "Could you do me a favor and help me with my math homework?"

Arnold is also in the ninth grade, only at a different private school. He goes to the Flemington School.

I ought to tell you that the one terrific thing about my gigantic apartment building on the West Side of New York City is that it has thirteen kids in the ninth grade. And that doesn't count the twin building next door.

We even put out our own gossip column.

Unfortunately, I'm usually in it with Arnold, a boy who is even more ordinary than I am. I'm in the gossip column with Arnold because Doris Kledge, the editor, likes to be fair and put everybody in, even those of us with zero social life. Our lines usually read something like, "Gilly Miles and Arnold Dorfenberg were seen doing homework together again. Gilly, you can say you're studying all you want, but we saw that math book was upside down. Kissy kissy!"

Don't get me wrong. I like Arnold. As a friend. He's not Shep Newman in my honors math class however. I've had a crush on Shep since first grade.

"Arnold . . . I'm locked out. I'm waiting for my mom. I'm tired. How can you ask about your homework?"

"I don't know. I just can."

If you look at Arnold's face, he has perfect features. Dark hair, light complexion, great nose. Blue eyes. But he lacks . . . charisma. Arnold has zero-minus-three charisma. With his glasses, he's down to zero-minus-four. And when he clears his throat all the time, he drops below minus six.

"Please Gil . . . I have a test tomorrow on rational numbers . . . just for a little while . . . till your mom comes. Please."

What can I say? "Sure."

I go back into the bedroom, explain the situation to Franny, and walk out with Arnold. We double-jump the stairs until we reach his apartment.

His mom is vacuuming in the living room.

"Hello, Mrs. Dorfenberg," I say.

"Hi, Gilly. How are you?"

Mrs. Dorfenberg says hello in that special voice she has when she speaks to me. It's a voice that drips with pity.

"How's your mom holding up, hmm?"

"She's fine, Mrs. Dorfenberg. Terrific, actually."

Which is a total lie. My mom's a mess. She used to be loads of fun, but she's been incredibly sad since my father dumped her. I wish I could make her happy and pretty again but I don't know how.

"Can I use the ladies' room, Mrs. Dorfenberg?"

"Of course!"

So I make a dash. I just stand in there and calm down. It upsets me to have to talk about my parents' divorce with people like Arnold's mom.

In three minutes there's a knock.

"You okay, Gil?" It's Arnold.

I open the door and come out.

"Yeah . . ."

"My mom didn't mean anything. She's a little dense. That's where I get my denseness from." He grins.

"I'm okay." And then we go into Arnold's room and do his math. It isn't easy. Arnold is not the smartest student in the world. Unlike Shep. Arnold is not the greatest athlete, unlike Shep. Arnold is not the greatest anything. He's just Arnold. Like I'm just Gilly.

As we finish and are closing our books, Mrs. Dorfenberg peeks her head into the room.

"Gilly . . . your mom's home."

As soon as she's out the door, I pile up my books and race down the stairs to my floor.

My door is slightly ajar and so is the door to Mrs. Hearn's apartment. I can hear voices inside. I run into my house, drop my stuff, and give my mom a big hug.

"Sorry I'm late, sweetie," she says. "I had extra typing. But I picked up some Chinese food for you and Jeff."

"That's okay, Mom. I think there are people looking at Mrs. Hearn's apartment. You want to come
out and spy on them?"

She laughs. Good. I like it when my mom laughs.

"Why don't you check them out," she says. "If they
take the apartment, let me know."

I quickly glance at the mail. Then I grab an apple and
run out.

In the hall is one of the weirdest-looking families
I've ever seen. There's a father, a bearded professor
type, a very plump mother type, and their daughter,
who is a head taller than me and wearing purple tights,
shorts, a khaki, buttoned shirt that says BRONX
ZOO ATTENDANT on one pocket, a comb in her
hair, and high buttoned boots. And in one hand is a little movie camera.

I nod shyly to each of them, one by one. Her parents
nod back. She sneezes. Then she belches.

"Victory!" her mother says.

"And God bless you," I add.

"Victory's my name," she says. "It's not a thing to
say after you belch." She grins and picks at her front
tooth. Her mother shakes her head and follows
Victory's father back into the apartment. She eyes
them carefully and then stares at me again.

"And what's your name?"

I clear my throat. "Uh . . . Gilly . . . Gilly Miles. Do
you . . . think you're going to be moving in?"

"Uh huh."

I point to her camera. "Are you uh . . . making a

movie or something . . . or is that your family's camera?"

"No, it's mine. I love movies. Right now I'm making a twenty-minute film about my life."

"Really? I've thought of being a filmmaker when I grow up too. My mom used to work in them before I was born."

"No kidding. Who do you like? Directorwise?"

"Oh . . . I like uh . . ." I know I shouldn't say Steven Spielberg or somebody new. I think of the two great old movies my mom just took me to at the Regency, a revival movie theater in my neighborhood. "Uh . . . Howard Harkes. Hawkes?"

She smiles, pleased. "Me too. Well, maybe you want to help me on this project . . ."

"Well . . . sure . . . uh . . . maybe . . ."

Now she stares at me. "In fact . . . you have an interesting face for film."

"I do?"

"Uh huh. Very gentle but . . . very deceptive."

"Huh?" I'm insulted.

"I don't mean deceptive bad. I mean deceptive like . . . intriguing. You look normal . . . regular . . . but there's something else underneath . . . mystery . . ."

"There is?"

She nods, moving her open hands in front of her like she's molding an imaginary sculpture.

"Like Greta Garbo—you know her? She was a movie star who was shy on the outside but dramatic and complex on the inside." She backs away from me. "In

11

fact . . . to tell you the truth, you remind me of myself
. . . on the inside . . ."

"Gee . . ."

"Yeah . . . you do." And then she flashes the warmest
dimpled grin.

I grin back.

Wow. She is something. She's so unusual!

And she thinks I am too.

Now, that's unusual!

Just then we hear the door to the stairs creak open.

Arnold peeks his head out into our hallway.

"Hi . . ." He smiles.

Victory's eyes widen. "Well . . . hello," she says in an
incredibly smoky voice.

Arnold turns suddenly into a statue, frozen with shyness. I know how he feels.

"Come on in," Victory says sexily. "Welcome to
our hallway."

He still doesn't move.

"Uh . . . Gilly . . . uh . . . I think you took my math
book."

"I did? I'll get it. I'll be back in a sec." And I make a
dash back into my apartment.

My mom is lying on the couch, the back of one hand
covering her forehead.

"Mom . . . did you see where I put my books?"

"They're right on the chair in the hallway."

"Right."

"So who moved in?"

"I can't describe it. You'd have to see her for yourself. You sure you don't want to come out and take a look?"

"Honey, I'd love to but I'm bushed."

My mom's been tired a lot lately, ever since she's taken this temporary typing job. She hates it but she says she needs to do it until she finds a good job. A career kind of job.

"Well, you rest, okay? I'll be back soon."

I rush back out to the hall.

Victory is still standing where she was. But now Arnold is standing beside her. Or, should I say, trembling beside her? She's caressing his Izod shirt with a finger.

"Arnold," I say. "Here's your book." He doesn't hear me.

"Arnold. Earth to Arnold. Come in."

They both turn around. Victory smiles.

Then she looks at Arnold, says, "Excuse me, cutie," to him, and walks halfway into our hall with me.

She gestures with a roll of her eyes back at him. He's shoving his glasses into his shirt pocket and blinking.

"Is he yours, Gilly?"

I shake my head no. I shake it emphatically.

"Good. I want him. He's gorgeous."

My mouth drops open and I try to hide that I am going into deep shock.

"You think he's a virgin?"

I almost choke on my apple. Which starts me to cough hysterically.

"Uh . . . there's a good chance that he is, yes . . ." I keep coughing.

Victory slaps my back, hard. And then she looks back at Arnold. He winks awkwardly, more like a series of nervous tics. Victory slowly and dramatically puts her hand on her lips and blows him a kiss.

Chapter 3

That *night my brother Jeff, Mom, and I sit around* our kitchen table, devouring the Chinese food. My mom always used to take the food out of the containers and put them in pretty bowls. She even lit candles that made the orange sauce shine just right. But lately even the containers look soggy and depressed.

She yawns.

"Sorry. So . . . then what happened?"

"Then Victory's parents shook the super's hand and said they'd move in on Sunday. Arnold was still standing there when I left."

Jeff shakes his head. "I don't get it. She's after Arnold Barfing Burger's body? Maybe she's with the sanitation department."

I had to laugh.

Jeff puts down his chopsticks. "What I want to know

15

is, why doesn't somebody worthwhile move in next door? Like a nude dancer or something."

"Cut it out. That's so sexist. Tell him to cut it out, Mom."

Unfortunately my mom can't do that. Because her eyes are closing. Jeff and I both look at her as she tucks her head into her arms and begins to nap on the kitchen table. We shake our heads.

"Poor Mom!" Jeff whispers.

I nod. "She's exhausted from that stupid boring typing. Ever since the separation . . ." I can't go on because I'm getting upset again. My mom is terrific and smart. She deserves a new career but she can't find one, and I think it's because she's still sad and can't get herself to really try.

I know she's still sad. Sometimes we'll watch a romantic movie on television, and tears will come to her eyes. But when she sees me staring, she puts on a big smile or leaves the room.

Jeff leans his head toward my face, with a sincere look. An older brother look. "Listen, Gilly . . . we have to talk."

I avoid his eyes. I know he's going to talk to me about my "attitude" problem with Morton Miles. Formerly known as Daddy.

"Gilly, Dad wants to see you. He misses you."

I shrug. "I just saw him. He and what's-her-name took me to see the Impressionists at the Metropolitan."

"That was a month ago. Gil . . . you have to give Abby a chance. She's nice. She's a nice person."

"I'm seeing him tomorrow at your thing. Unless

16

you'll let me miss it. I'll do alternate service. I'll clean your room. I'll do your math."

"You do *my* math?" He stops himself. Sometimes Jeff just can't help being an egomaniac. He's good-looking and vice president of his class. And he just got into Harvard early admission.

He is also Franny's Master X.

Jeff puts his hand over mine. "Gilly, you know I start living with Dad next week."

"Just Monday through Thursdays . . ."

"They want you to come too. By law, they could make you come. The divorce called for split custody."

"Forget it, Jeff! I said I'd never go to his house again and I meant it."

"Did you ever think Mom might want you to try it? She talks to Abby."

"No way!"

Maybe my mom could use a break, but how could I live with Dad as though he were a nice guy?

Before Airhead moved in, that was hard enough.

But with Airhead. Forget it.

The last time I was there, she screamed at me just because I said I didn't like pot roast.

It wasn't personal. I hate all pot roast. Hers was probably no worse than any other.

What happened was we were all sitting at her table. And she got up and said, "And now, Gilly . . . for a very special meal. One of your favorite foods."

"Lobster?" I asked.

"Uh uh," she said.

"Uh . . . shrimp?" I asked.

"Uh . . . uh . . ."

"What then? Mexican? Chinese? Sushi?"

She shook her head every time.

And then she went into the kitchen and brought out this platter and said: "Tadaaa . . . brisket!"

"Yech" just came out of my mouth. I couldn't help it.

Maybe if she hadn't introduced it that way and got my hopes up . . .

Well, she was furious. She gave this speech about how we must all be polite to each other and then screamed at my father, "I don't need this!" and ran right out of the room.

And then I said, "I don't need this either."

And I left.

The next day my dad called and said it was a misunderstanding. Airhead had asked him, "Does Gilly like brisket?" and he wasn't really listening or was trying to be nice and answered, "She loves it." And it was all his fault, he said.

That's for sure.

I hate going there. And I'm never going back. I know my father and my mother and Abigail speak to each other about it. Somehow my mom puts up with those phony polite conversations. But I won't do it!

Just then the phone rings.

I beat Jeff to the receiver.

It's Doris Kledge.

"Hi, Doris. Yeah . . . Yeah . . . How'd you hear about it so fast?"

Unbelievable. She's already heard about my new neighbor, Victory Norton.

I listen to Doris's deep alto voice.

"Are you ready, Gilly? This is my lead item for tomorrow's issue of *West End Avenue Winds*. Are you ready?"

"I'm ready, Doris."

Doris clears her throat and recites: "What whiz kid has been taking a certain Arnold Somebody for granted so that he has just been snatched from under her pencil by a new femme fatale who is moving into our humble building?"

I can't believe it. "Doris," I say, "if you print that, I'll sue your father's dry-cleaning store for every suit he's ever pressed."

"I heard it from a very reliable source. You can't sue me if I'm printing the truth."

"Doris," I say, "I want my subway-map T-shirt back. Tonight!"

"So big deal. I'll give it back." She pauses. "I thought it was written rather well."

And she hangs up.

Fabulous. What a day. I never liked Arnold *that way*. The boyfriend way. And now Doris has him dumping me.

I stood there and thought about it a second.

And who could she have heard this ridiculous gossip from?

Who else?

Arnold, of course.

I'm going to kill him.

Chapter 4

The next morning, as Franny and I walk out of our dark lobby to meet the other kids waiting on the stoop, the sun hits us with light. It's a beautiful March day.

"I mean, I can't believe it. She's sexy and she likes Arnold?" Franny says.

"Uhuh. Weird, right? You should have seen him, too. He was bewitched. He actually looked taller by the time she finished with him. She's really interesting."

"Really?"

"She really is. Like she makes movies. And now she's shooting a movie of her whole life. And she actually asked me to help her. Wouldn't that be exciting?"

Franny shrugs. "Could be. . . . Are you going to?"

"Maybe. I've always wanted to make movies. I'll bet you could help too."

"True . . ." Franny's voice relaxes. "You should have knocked on my door and introduced me."

"I should have."

"Although"—Franny makes a face—"she sounds punk. I hate punk."

"She's not. She's just unusual. Creative. Unconventional. She's got charisma."

"I get it, Gilly. I get it."

I look at Franny's face but she looks away. I detect a hint of jealousy, so I add, "I mean, I could never be 'friendsfriends' with her, like us." I smile reassuringly.

She shrugs. "I don't care." But I feel Franny relax a little more.

I guess even somebody as confident as Franny needs a little reassurance.

As soon as we reach the front stoop, the rest of the girls nod. But we don't stop to talk. We automatically start to walk. It's like this unspoken thing. Like a machine which starts as soon as all its parts are in place.

Actually, it's like the kicking formation of the New York Jets. Because there are eleven of us. And we walk six girls across in the first row, three or four girls behind them and a couple behind them. We all go to different schools, but we walk together every morning.

I stick to the second row, on the outside, next to Franny.

In the front row, center, is Tamara Apthorp. Black hair and eyes. Beautiful. She goes to Dalton, a very good private school. She's rich rich rich. She's not really a friend. But everybody likes her. Next to Tamara is Toby Konig. Toby is short and cute. But not as cute as she thinks she is. My mom is always saying to me,

21

"Gilly, you should have more confidence in yourself." Her mom should say to her, "Toby, honey . . . you should have *less* confidence in yourself."

Next to her is Ronnie Simon, who goes to Barrow with Franny, Toby, and me. Ronnie is great. She's pretty. But not too pretty. She's smart, but not too smart. She has only one bad habit. She hates grease. She hates anything with fat on it. Every day in the lunchroom, Ronnie degreases her hamburger by laying her napkin on top of it. It can make you ill.

In the back row are the Belson twins. They go to Flemington. Next to them is Loraine Mayers, who goes to public school and is a genius, and Doris Kledge. Doris is handing out her scandal sheet as we walk.

Luckily, as soon as Franny reads it, she says, "Gee, Doris, you're never gonna work for the *Times*. You know Gilly and Arnold are just good friends. What you're doing is called libel . . . and news distortion. In the world of media, it's considered to be bad form . . . we could sue you."

Doris looks at Franny. "*West End Avenue Winds* is a gossip column. It's not supposed to be the front page of the *Times*. It's supposed to be trashy. Just because somebody has no sense of humor. . . ." She pauses. "And, frankly, my father says there's no such thing as a simple friendship between a man and a woman. I rest my case."

Ronnie turns around and looks at Doris. "Doris . . . you're such a jerk. Stuff it."

That's what I mean. Ronnie is terrific.

But Toby butts in. "Frankly," she says, "I don't know

why you're so upset, Gilly. You and Arnold might still get back together. This girl sounds much too mature for Arnold. And you and he were made for each other."

I guess Toby is trying to be nice in a condescending kind of way . . . but I consider it insulting. I don't mean to be a snob about Arnold, but, well, I deserve a boyfriend better than him. Why does everybody see me as so ordinary?

Wait'll I win the Nobel Prize for Literature. Or cure cancer. Wait'll some Hollywood star falls in love with me. Or Shep asks me for a date.

Or it's ninety degrees in the winter.

Who am I kidding?

We reach 84th Street.

"Okay, fellow Barrow-inians," Ronnie says. "This is where we get off."

Franny, Ronnie, Toby Konig, and I turn up 84th Street toward Central Park West.

The four of us walk for a while.

They ask me questions about Victory and I try to answer them.

"I mean, how different can she be from everybody else? She's not punk. She's not an intellectual. She's not a jock. She's not a rocker. What could she be?"

"That's the thing. She's hard to categorize . . . she's—"

And just as I'm about to find the word, we arrive at the steps of the Barrow School, the only school in New York that could go bankrupt. Standing there, waving at me with great—and loud—enthusiasm, is none other than Victory Norton.

Chapter 5

*S*he runs toward us, hugs me, and plants a loud and squeaky kiss on each cheek.

"I may go here!" she says. "We're taking the tour this morning."

I look over at the entrance. The Nortons are standing there, waiting for Victory. As usual they look annoyed at their daughter.

"What's wrong? What'd you do?" I ask her.

"They don't like what I'm wearing."

I look at her outfit. She is all dressed up for the day. Nice tweed coat, respectable jumper and shoes.

"Why? It's practically prep school. And that jumper is a great color on you."

"That's what I said, too."

Franny, who is standing beside us, is staring at Victory. She hesitates and then says, "Yeah . . . it's a great color, but . . . but it's a . . . a . . ."

Victory finishes the sentence. "It's a maternity dress." She winks. "I'm not pregnant. I picked it up in a thrift shop. These things are worn for a few months, so they're practically new. I hate waste." She turns around to model the jumper. "Don't you love it?"

At this point Toby and Ronnie move toward us and are gaping.

"My parents think it makes a bad impression to wear a maternity dress when you go to a new school," Victory says. "But I don't think they'll notice. Only fashion types are gonna notice."

I could feel Franny flinch.

Victory looks at her.

"Sorry . . . I didn't mean that in a bad way."

"That's okay. No problem." Franny smiles. Franny never loses her cool.

Ronnie immediately says, "Don't worry about the maternity dress, Victory. Barrow is a progressive school. They don't care. They'll take anybody."

"Yeah," Toby adds. "You could probably wear a topless dress if you can pay cash."

"I don't want to say the school is broke," Ronnie says, "but in bio last week, four of us had to share the same paramecium."

Victory laughs.

"Great." Victory smiles warmly at everybody. "I really want to go here, but my parents heard you don't learn anything."

"Sure we do," I say. "We just can't remember it long."

I made up that joke fast, but actually, insults about Barrow hurt. Okay, it may not be a "great" school, and I know progressive schools aren't fashionable these days. But I've been going here since I was four. I love the place.

"You mean, practically whatever I do, they won't kick me out?" Victory asks.

"Well, not exactly," Franny says. "You can argue about anything. You can wear anything. You can call teachers by their first names. But you can't be fresh." She pauses, staring at Victory. "We even have a great girls' basketball team. You play?"

Victory shakes her head and makes a face.

"I'm opposed to anything where you wear a uniform. Plus . . . basketball is for preppy types who are trying to get extracurricular stuff so they can get into Brown or Yale."

Franny says quietly, "I'm captain of the team." She pauses. "Too bad you feel that way. We could use someone like you. Someone . . . hefty."

Victory stares right at Franny, smiles and says, "Well, I'd love to stay and chat but I only have one minute." And she sticks up her middle finger at Franny to indicate the number one!

I don't think Franny and Victory and I are going to be best friends.

There is so much tension all of a sudden that Ronnie starts to hum. She does that when she's nervous.

"Well," I say, trying to be peacemaker, "you can be anything you want at Barrow. There's room for everybody."

But Franny just stands there. And so does Victory.

26

After a second, Franny speaks. "Right," she says. "Whatever you do at Barrow's okay ... within the bounds of good taste."

Uh oh.

Victory picks right up on that one. "Good taste? What's that?"

Franny responds calmly. "Maybe you'll find out." She has such a sweet smile on her face that my face could break out just looking at it.

Franny retosses her scarf and puts her arm in mine.

"Well ... we gotta go," she says. "Barrow is very strict when you're more than a half hour late."

Then her voice gets sort of formal. "Hope you come to Barrow, Victory." And she starts toward the entrance, taking my arm, which is attached to my body, with her.

Somehow it seems rude to just leave, so I remove my arm and stand there. Franny keeps walking, her elbow still out. I can't see it but I know that her face is red.

"Franny is sooo great," I start to blabber as we stare. "Believe me, you're gonna love her ..." My voice kind of trails off, because Victory is not even listening. She is staring at the door that Franny has just walked through.

"I'm sure she's nice," she says. "It's just obvious that she's so different"—she pauses, linking our arms— "from us."

Chapter 6

*B*y the time I enter the main lobby, Franny is gone. So I climb the back stairs to my floor.

When I reach the third floor, I pass Gerry, my homeroom and English teacher, standing in the hall, talking to Mike, the gym teacher. They're in love.

In our room, Gregory Chasen, the funniest kid in our class, is standing in front of the blackboard, imitating Jessica Parrington, the richest kid in our class.

"My daahlings," Gregory is saying in a fancy voice, "we must have a paaty at my summer place before Dadda and Mummy close the house. Wouldn't that be divine? Now, Jennifer, you come and bring the designer paper plates, and Leora, you bring the designer napkins, and Sharia, you bring . . . hmm . . . would you happen to know if there's such a thing as designer potato chips?"

Everybody bursts out laughing just as Gerry walks in.

"Good morning, Gerry," Gregory says. And slides quickly into his first-row seat.

At Barrow we call the teachers by their first names. My father hates that, of course. I love it.

Just as Gerry begins to take attendance, we hear the static of the loudspeaker, and then the voice of our principal, Miriam Buckenoff.

"Good morning, Barrow students. This is Miriam."

The whole class now stares at the speaker on the wall. I look at Franny, but she looks away.

"I'm addressing you all this morning for several reasons. I want all of you to remind your parents to fill in the auction flyer donating either goods or services for auction night."

I nudge Franny. She doesn't smile back.

"And I would like to inform you that because of a slight cash-flow problem, Barry, our assistant custodial engineer, will be departing. We will be depending on Jack and Tom to carry the burden."

Everybody looks at each other and giggles. Barrow Financial Crisis #57.

Miriam continues.

"Finally, I want to assure you that despite the rumors, Barrow is doing just fine. To paraphrase Mark Twain, the news of our death has been greatly exaggerated. We are alive and well. That is not to say that we are not experiencing some financial stress. There will be continued sacrifices. Therefore, I also want to report that the Board of Directors, in another belt-tightening move, has decided to pay for the new computers—by eliminating lunchroom hot-meal service."

The whole class bursts into applause.

"I hope that is not an inconvenience for anybody."

Throughout the halls you can hear kids shouting "No!" or "We'll manage!" or "There is a God!"

Everybody's laughing.

Barrow is a little strange. It's true, it is broke. And it's true, for an expensive school, it's been forced to cut down on certain services. And maybe we don't learn as many facts as I will have to learn next year if I get into Bronx Science, but it's still a great place. At least, to kids. It's like a home. Not a school maybe—but a home.

I look at Franny, trying to share this typical silly Barrow moment. But she still won't look at me.

While I'm looking, Victory passes us in the hall. She waves. But her parents are shaking their heads. And putting on their coats.

"I think we just lost another student," I say to no one in particular.

Franny finally turns around. "Such a shame," she responds.

Chapter 7

My mom and I are walking home from Broadway, where we've just bought me a pair of shoes for tonight's "festivities." They're ugly. My mom has no sense of style lately. That's one of the things she has to change if she's going to find a real career.

"Look, Gil, I'm sure Franny won't stay mad. Victory did sound a bit obnoxious. But so did she."

"I know."

My mom looks at me with a tiny scowl.

"Don't forget your old friends, Gil, just because something new comes along. Unless . . . unless you really don't like Franny anymore. . . ."

"Ma, of course I do! She's my best friend. She's great. Sure, sometimes we are a little bored with each other, but we've known each other so long. I would never throw that away. Never."

Never. I believe in loyalty. For friends, for my school, for anything I love.

My father and I used to talk about this stuff all the time. Loyalty. How people should behave. What being a "good" person was.

We talked about it a lot. Until he walked out on us.

"Well," my mom says, "when we get home, go into Franny's and talk it out."

"I can't. She's at practice. And we're probably going to Bronx Science before she gets back. But we're supposed to go shopping tomorrow . . . if she'll talk to me."

Just then I spot Arnold Dorfenberg coming toward us.

"Hi!" He waves to me. "I got to talk to you." He has a panicky look on his face. But I don't wave back. I remember the gossip he gave to Doris Kledge.

"I'm busy, Arnold," I say. "See me when I've got more time. Like when I'm an adult."

"I'm sorry about the column, Gilly. Really. Doris forced it out of me. Anyway . . . anyway . . ." He looks at my mom. My mom smiles. "Good morning, Mrs. Miles," he says, trying to look calm. "You're looking very well."

My mom knows something's up so she says, "Gilly . . . would you mind walking ahead with Arnold? I forgot I have to pick up some milk and juice."

Arnold smiles at my mom gratefully. And then pulls my elbow till we're walking alone. The panic is right back on his face.

"Gilly, Victory saw the column! It practically says she's a slut. She called me."

"Arnold, you deserve it. It didn't exactly make me sound like Miss Popularity, either. You can't do that to people."

"I know. But Doris made me." Now he takes out the column. It's folded about thirty-six times. He unfolds it and reads: "'We hear that the whole G line is complaining to the Dorfenbergs. It seems that Young Arnold is constantly using up water taking cold showers!!! Or are we all wet about that?'"

He takes a deep breath.

"I'm not really upset about the column," Arnold says. "It's Victory."

"She really got mad, huh?" I say.

"Well . . . uh . . . not exactly. That's the problem. She loved it!"

"Of course!" I say. "That's Victory!"

I really do want to be her friend.

Arnold grabs my sleeve. He continues in an urgent voice as we go into our building.

"When she called, her voice was so sexy that my mom thought a grown woman was after me. My mom was so upset, she made my dad talk to me about sex. What does my dad know about sex? He's an accountant."

I do my best not to laugh. I fail.

Arnold gets upset. "Gilly . . . listen. This is serious. She asked me out for tonight! I said yes. And she expects . . . you know . . . some action. And . . . and . . . I'm not . . . I'm not as experienced as you might think I am."

"Arnold . . . what does this have to do with me?"

33

"Well . . . would you think I was totally crazy . . . if I asked you if we could . . . practice? Just kissing. Nothing else."

Arnold was right. He was crazy.

"Arnold . . . you're asking me to kiss you so you can kiss another girl? I mean that is so gross . . . so insulting . . . so demeaning."

"I'll pay."

"Get outta here."

He shakes his head.

"I know it sounds bad, but . . . I'm fourteen years old and I've never . . . I haven't engaged in heavy sex in quite a few years."

"Is that a fact?" I say sarcastically.

"Thanks a lot, Gilly. You're my oldest friend. When I was three days old, your carriage was next to my carriage in the park. And what do I get for it now, I ask you? What do I get for sharing my life with you? Sarcasm."

At this point I'm not even listening, he is being so ridiculous, so . . . so Arnold.

Then he stops walking and looks at me. On his face is honest fear.

"You know, Gilly . . . I know I'm a boy and I'm supposed to jump at this chance but . . ." He looks at me and it bursts out: "I can't handle it. Really. I want to . . . I want her to like me so bad. But . . . I'm gonna look like a fool."

"Arnold . . . can't you practice on a doll or something?"

"I tried. But the lips don't move. I know she does stuff with her mouth. She's the type."

He looks so sad that I put an arm around his shoulder.

"Arnold," I say, "I know you're scared, but at least you're going to do it tonight. You're going to have some fun. Some experience. That's more than I can say. Enjoy it, Arnold. You'll be fine. You're nervous now, but you'll be fine!" I swallow hard so I can get out this lie: "You're a very handsome and sexy guy. Victory couldn't resist you."

I stare at my new purple shoes so he can't tell my face is contorting from that ridiculous statement. But he doesn't even notice.

"You really think so?" he says. "I'm beginning to think so too, but most people don't . . . think so."

"I know so, Arnold." I try to look at him like he was a sex symbol.

He sighs. "Thanks, Gilly. I owe you one."

"Good luck," I say.

"Thanks. And good luck to you, too. You're seeing your dad tonight at the Science Fair, right?"

I nod.

"I hope it goes okay. I really do."

We're standing on the landing between his floor and mine. Now he looks at me. So relieved. And suddenly he takes my shoulders in his hands, pulls me toward him . . . and kisses me. A long kiss. On the mouth.

And all of a sudden I feel this extremely warm feeling inside. This little . . . expanding . . . bubble.

I put my hands on his chest as he looks at me. I look at him. He smiles back. And then he releases my shoulders and runs up the stairs toward his floor.

I just stand there, a little woozy. A little . . . shocked.

Arnold's face suddenly appears before me again as he jumps back down a few of the steps.

"That was a nice kiss, Gilly. Did you like it?"

I'm still just standing there, still feeling this funny feeling. But I nod.

And then he runs up to the next landing again. And shouts as he runs, "That's a relief! I guess I have nothing to worry about for tonight."

Arnold. He is incredible.

I'm sure this sensation is nothing. Probably just a severe case of kiss deprivation. I've been kissless for so long.

Still . . . I have the funniest feeling.

And I'm going to stop feeling it as fast as I can.

Chapter 8

*T*he cabdriver who took my mom, Jeff, and me up to Jeff's school was such a lunatic that I thought I might be lucky and not have to see my father and Abigail tonight. I'd be in a hospital emergency room instead. But we made it.

Now we're standing outside the Bronx High School of Science. It's an enormous modern building that holds around three thousand students from every country in the world. And they're all very smart.

Lots of people are milling around outside and inside the doors too. None of them are my father. Yet.

As soon as we walk inside, three kids whisk Jeff away.

"Why don't we find a seat in the auditorium? Get up close," I ask my mother nervously.

"Fine," she says. "As long as we save two seats for your father and Abigail."

"Of course. But if they don't come soon, it's rude to save seats so long."

My mother doesn't fall for it. "Then we'll wait here for them," she says. "We are going to sit with them, Gil, so just accept it."

We look at each other. I know my mother's nervous too.

I look at her more closely. She should have worn more makeup. She doesn't look so great.

I stare at the door, looking for my father and Abigail, while hundreds of parents and relatives come in. My stomach is doing flips. I pray that their car broke down, that they overslept ten hours, that they got the night wrong, that they broke up on the way over.

I'm just going to be calm. And polite. If that's what the witch wants, politeness, that's what the witch is going to get.

Then the door opens and in they come. Abigail leads the way. She makes Christie Brinkley look like a bag lady. Even in dungarees, with legs that never end, and a loose shirt, she's gorgeous. When she sees us, she waves and smiles widely. Like her commercials.

My father waves and smiles narrowly. He's nervous too.

Naturally Abigail's first words after hellos are, "Well, you must be very proud of your brother!"

I want to say, "What do you care?" But all I do is nod and agree. "Yes," I say, "I am very proud. And how are you? I saw you on TV . . ." And all that garbage.

My father just stands there staring at me. I avoid his

eyes as long as possible, but then Jeff walks over, says, "Mom . . . Abigail . . ." and takes the two of them away.

"Hold it!" I start to say. But they keep going and my father grabs my arm.

I panic. "Uh . . . I have to go to the ladies' room . . ."

"Gilly . . . I want to talk to you. Please. Abby and I are going up to a tennis camp in the Berkshires next weekend. We'd love to have you come. We'd like to talk to you. What do you say?"

He knows I love tennis. But if I have to talk to Abigail in order to get to play tennis, I'll give up tennis.

"Well, that sounds very nice, Dad. But . . . I'm not sure. I mean . . . it's really thoughtful of you. Can I think about it?"

He nods and stares at me again until he snares my eyes with his. We make contact. And he says, "I miss you terribly, Gilly. You know that. What happened, happened. Everybody's sorry about it."

I look away.

It's hard to keep being phony when someone else is being sincere.

Suddenly I see a little white mouse scurrying down the corridor. After a second it turns and runs back toward me. Then it reaches a wall . . . sniffs . . . and turns again. And scurries away.

From the end of the long hallway we hear a girl wailing.

"I'm through. My life is over. If anything happened to Checkerboard, I'll die!"

My father and I look at each other, startled.

Then a mother's voice sssshes the girl's voice.

"Calm down, Stacy . . . calm down. Let's not make a

mountain out of a molehill. No mouse is that important . . ."

The girl starts crying. "Not that important? He's my whole project! I can't believe it. You're the one who wants me to get into Brown. Oh, God! Checkerboard, where are you?"

I spot Checkerboard slipping under the WELCOME PARENTS sign which hangs from a long table. But as I walk toward him, the little guy runs right out from behind the sign. Then he spots me. His tiny black eyes dart around. He stares at me, paralyzed with fear.

(I mean, I don't *know* that he's paralyzed with fear. I'm guessing.)

I'm kind of paralyzed too when my dad shouts, "Stay there, Gilly! Just start moving slowly toward him . . . and me."

The mouse is now between me and my dad, so I move toward it a half step at a time.

"That's it, Gil. Thatta girl."

But suddenly Checkerboard dashes past me before I can catch him. He reaches the far wall, stops again, and pivots. And then runs toward me again. And past me, right into my father's large hands.

My dad scoops him up, but as he's raising the mouse to waist level the little guy wiggles out and drops to the floor. Luckily, I instinctively move toward him and he runs right back to my father.

My dad raises him gently this time, kisses him on the fur, and hands him to me.

My father's and my eyes meet. We smile at each other.

Now, as we stand, I'm holding the mouse in my

hands, petting its soft white fur. The girl, still crying, reaches me and spots the mouse in my hands. I hold it out to her.

"Oh, thank God! Thank you. Thank God. Thank you. You saved my life. My mouse. Everything!"

"It's no big deal," I say.

"Yes, it is," she says. "Thank you. Thank you."

It's nice to be thanked thirteen times.

The girl takes the mouse, starting to explain. "You see, Checkerboard's my prize mouse. We injected her with methyl bidioxysilicate, mated her with black mice, and produced alternating generations of black and white mice with the checkerboard pattern on the exterior lateral side. Not only did I win first prize tonight, but Dr. Lawrence in the Bio Department wants me to enter the Westinghouse Science Fair with her. I mean, if anything had happened . . ."

I nod. I don't know what to say since I don't understand a word she said.

"Well . . . that's great," I fumble. "Fascinating."

Her mother nods in agreement.

My father reaches over to pet the mouse. I indicate him with my thumb. "Actually, my father's the one who really caught her."

The man is a louse and a homewrecker but he did save this mouse.

The girl gives my dad a peck on the cheek.

Then her mother practically bats her eyes at my father and says, "Aren't you wonderful."

Even the girl genius is embarrassed. "Well, Mom," she murmurs. "We better go." And yanks her away.

41

Leaving my father and me alone together again.

My father grins. "It's fun to be a hero, even if all you save's a mouse, isn't it, Gil?"

I nod.

"We better go in." And he puts his arm around me as we start toward the auditorium.

I'm getting this warm, loving feeling. Like no time has gone by between my dad and me. No divorce. Like he didn't take a little family in his hands and crush it to death when he moved in with the wicked witch. Like I'm just a little girl and the man with his arm around me is my daddy. Like the old days. I look at him.

But I won't forget. I won't forgive him.

I won't!

I want to scream. I want to scream, "I hate you for what you did!" But all I do is wiggle out of his grasp, shove his arm away, and say, as politely as I can muster, "Yes. Mother and Airhead must be waiting for us in the auditorium. So let's go in . . . shall we?"

Chapter 9

*I*t's eleven o'clock in the morning and I've been up since five. I couldn't sleep. I put a croissant in the toaster.

The rest of the evening was a disaster that got worse.

My father was furious at me for calling Abigail "Airhead."

I sat on the other side of my mother and didn't say a word to him for the rest of the night. I spoke only through my mother.

It was very uncomfortable and I felt like an idiot.

The only good thing was that at six o'clock this morning I put a note under Franny's door telling her my evening was terrible and to pick me up when she was ready to go out. I figure sympathy for my life will distract her from being mad at me.

It's funny how you can feel two things at the same time. Miserable and . . . calculating.

The toaster oven pops open and I start to butter my croissant when I hear four knocks on my door, to the beat of Beethoven's Fifth Symphony.

Knock-knock knock knahhhhhhk.

That could only be Arnold.

I let him in.

I am immediately aware that as I look at him, I feel two things about him too. As he pushes his glasses up his nose, he's the same old shleppy Arnold. But he also looks handsome to me.

He gives me the high-five sign. And as we clasp hands at the end of it, I feel a flutter again.

This is ridiculous. I'm going to fight this feeling if it's the last thing I do.

Anyway, from the looks of things, he now belongs to Victory. He is positively euphoric, bounces down on a dining room chair, and stares at the croissant I'm nibbling on. He's wearing a green T-shirt with brown gravy stains.

"So . . . how'd it go?" I force myself to ask him.

He says the next words slowly and dramatically: "Faaaa . . . bulous . . . Just fab . . . ulous. And she's going to call here in about ten minutes."

"Ah-ha," I say matter-of-factly. "I think I need some jelly on this croissant. Would you mind getting it? It's on the second shelf in the fridge."

"Sure, my friend, my neighbor, my pal. I'll have one too, okay?"

He looks at me, waiting for another question. I refuse to give him the satisfaction. Besides not knowing exactly how I feel about him, it's hard to be happy for somebody else when you're feeling lousy.

Arnold doesn't notice. He just keeps talking.

"I really want to thank you about yesterday. Because I was great. Not only did we . . . you know . . . do a lot . . . but she read me this Dylan Thomas poem about two young lovers who defy the meaninglessness of existence by making out. I mean, you know, by necking they give life meaning." He sighs. "She's . . . so great. Just being with her, I feel different. I feel wiser." He holds up a jar of blueberry preserves. "How do you twist this cap off?"

"You figure it out, O great wise one." An angry feeling is starting to creep into my shoulders and neck. He hasn't even asked me about my night.

"Not only that, she's moving in tomorrow. She likes you a lot. She thinks you're a serious person with good values. She liked your aura."

That's great. I want Victory to like me. And my aura, whatever that is.

She's so interesting and she actually thinks I am too.

"We're going to an antinuke rally today and then down to Olden Camera to buy film for the movie. She wants you to come too. You know, Gil, she thinks you should actually act in this film!"

"Really?"

"Yeah. I told her forget it. You're shy. Timid. Not the daring type."

"Thanks a lot, Arnold."

"Gee, Gil—I'm just repeating what you say about

yourself. You're always telling me what a coward you are. . . . If she asks, you'd say no, wouldn't you?"

"Maybe. Maybe not."

Of course I'd normally say no. He's right. I'm not the actress type.

But this morning I feel so . . . fed up with myself.

The phone rings and I pick it up as fast as I can. My mom and Jeff are still asleep. They were talking about me till very late.

"Hello," I say.

It's Victory.

"Hi, Gil. Listen, Gil, did Arnold speak to you? I want you to be in my movie. What do you say?"

I'm tired of saying no when I really want to say yes.

"Yeah, he told me, Victory. And yes. Definitely yes. Definitely . . . maybe yes."

Arnold laughs.

And shouts into the phone, "She'll never do it. Never!"

I swat him away with the receiver.

"I'll do it, Victory. I'll do it!"

"Great! It's going to have everything. Sex. Violence. Sex."

Oh, God. What have I gotten myself into?

"Gilly . . . Gilly . . ."

The receiver is so far away I can barely hear Victory, so I bring it back to my ear. Just as I do, the door opens and Franny walks right in. She's smiling. That's good.

I wave to Franny as I listen to Victory ask me if she should pick me up for an antinuke rally she and Arnold are going to.

"Uh . . . I can't."

"Really? What can be more important than world peace?"

Franny slaps me on the back. "Morning, Gilly. Morning, Arnold. So . . . are you ready for Bloomingdale's?"

I clamp my hand over the receiver just as she says "Bloomingdale's." I shhhsh Franny and continue to talk on the phone.

"Uh . . . well, actually, Victory, I'm going to a . . . uh, woman's gathering. It's a chance . . . a time for women to get together and do what they really like to do . . . I don't know if you're into that . . ."

Victory's voice sounds very supportive. "Sure. Hey . . . that's great."

"Well . . . I've got to get off. I'll see you tomorrow when you move in. Arnold? . . . Sure. Hold on."

I hand him the phone.

Arnold puts the receiver to his ear and listens. He blushes, then takes the phone, walks into the closet with it, and closes the door.

We immediately hear loud puckering noises coming from between our overcoats.

Franny looks at the closet, looks at me.

"It's just Victory," I say, trying to make that fact seem unbelievably unimportant.

"How was last night, Gil?" she asks. "It didn't sound so good."

"It was terr-ible," I say. "And . . . I don't know . . . something's going on. My father actually called last night at midnight. And Jeff spoke to him. And my mother."

I'm about to go on, but Arnold now comes out of the closet, puts the receiver on the hook, and reaches for another croissant.

"She's wonderful. And she thinks that I, Arnold Dorfenberg the First . . . have it. You know what I'm talking about: it!" He now takes a huge bite of a croissant and then loudly licks his fingers.

Franny stares at him. She's never seen Arnold this way before.

"What's 'it,' Arnold?" she asks. "And if it's the flu, don't touch my glass."

Arnold shakes his head from left to right. "It," he says, "is sexual charisma, Franny. Body heat." And then, as he walks to the door: "And, by the way . . . could you do me a favor? From now on, call me Arn. I prefer it."

As the door slams, Franny mutters after him, affectionately, "Is he a nerd or is he a nerd? He is just perfect for Victory Norton."

She laughs. I don't.

"Hey. Gil . . . last night was that bad?" She shakes her head and looks at me with sympathy.

I nod.

"You want to talk about it?"

I shake my head.

"I understand, Gil. I really do." She puts her hand on my shoulder and goes on: "As you know, there are only two ways to improve your mental health under these circumstances. A good heart-to-heart talk in which you get all the bad stuff off your chest and reach some understanding of your innermost feelings." She pauses. "Or shopping."

She looks at me.

"What'll it be?"

"What do you think?" I say. "Let's go to Bloomingdale's!"

Chapter 10

We're sitting at the counter of a little coffee shop in Bloomingdale's basement, sharing a tuna sandwich and resting. And talking.

We spent the morning shopping. We covered three floors, and Franny helped me pick out a great peach skirt and blouse.

If there's a gene for shopping, Franny has it.

She also helped me pick out the prettiest ceramic earrings and a new key chain for my keys that glows in the dark.

"Well, I feel better. Much better!" I say, looking at the sleeve of the new blouse which I'm now wearing.

"Good." Franny nods and then stares at me closely. She fumbles in her pocketbook, studies me again, and then lifts a few strands of my curly mop. Pulling them back from my face, she clips on an adorable peach barrette.

"Peach is your color, Gil. Never forget that."

I take the little mirror she holds out to me.

It looks terrific.

I nod appreciatively and go back to nibbling on my half of the sandwich.

Franny is such a good friend.

True, all we do together is talk or play "Who Shall I Marry?" or shop. True, she's not as interesting as Victory, but she's such a good friend.

I'd like to look like Franny, but think like Victory.

I'd like to be sweet and kind like Franny—but daring and passionate like Victory.

I'd like to fly in the face of conformity like Victory, but . . . be as popular as Franny.

How can I talk this way?

I can't be someone else. I have to be myself.

But the thing is, who? When I'm with Franny, I love to shop. When I think of Victory, shopping seems so shallow. When I talk to Victory, I want to be creative and arty. When I'm with Franny, all that seems so phony.

We sit silently for a minute and then Franny looks at me again.

"You know, Gil, what I think? I think that if Abigail's a total dork, it's also true that your father chose her. They're meant for each other, he's a dork too, and your mom's well rid of him. But your mom's gonna be all right. She needs a job—and maybe some new clothes—but she'll be okay."

"I hope so." Why do I feel slightly uptight when Franny insults my dad? I know he deserves it, but I don't want her to go on with it.

"Listen, Fran," I say. "Uh . . . I need to talk to you . . . about Victory."

"I know, Gil. Look, I realize I overreacted yesterday."

"You did? You do?"

She nods.

I smile at her. "Well . . . it was awkward . . . it was. But she's moving in tomorrow. Maybe you could give her one more chance. For me?"

Franny half nods. And we just sit there. Relieved.

"You know, this weird thing happened yesterday," I say, changing the subject before Franny changes her mind. I look at my shopping bag, the sugar bowl on the counter, my Coke, as I speak.

"I . . . uh . . . I kissed Arnold . . ."

Franny looks at me, shocked.

"It was an accident. It was a total accident. But . . . uh . . . I felt something."

"You're kidding!"

I shake my head sadly.

Franny nods thoughtfully, then looks up at me.

"I don't think you should worry about it, Gil. It's probably nothing. It's our age. You'd feel something if you kissed Kermit the frog."

We laugh. I'm so relieved.

She continues. "Arnold is not cool enough for you, believe me. You deserve a guy like Shep. Like I deserve Master X. We both deserve the best."

See, that's the thing about Franny. She thinks I can be as cool as she is.

And yet Victory thinks I can be as ... well, passionate as Victory is.

It's weird really. They both think I'm like them.

You know why? Because I have no personality of my own.

It's awful. I'm just a piece of walking, breathing Silly Putty.

Franny gets up.

"I'm ready. Let's go back to the West Side and stop at the American. Have a sundae. What do you think?"

I get up. "Sounds like a great idea to me, Fran!"

The American Restaurant is a Greek coffee shop that serves great Italian pizza and French ice cream. Lots of the kids we know hang out there on Saturdays.

When we get there, we find a back booth and each order a triple hot-fudge Ben and Jerry's chocolate ice cream sundae topped with homemade gooey walnuts and mounds of real whipped cream. Real quality junk.

Franny skims a milliliter of hot fudge from her sundae.

She is such a slow eater. I purposely have stopped eating because otherwise I'll finish mine in three minutes and then I'll have to sit and watch her eat and want a sundae all over again.

"I have an interview at the Friends' School," she says. "I'm nervous about it."

"I know. But you have nothing to worry about. Any

school will want you. You're a good student, vice president of the class, you did well on the admission test . . . you should do great."

"I guess so. But interviews are scary."

I nod.

"Scary for you! If I had to do it, I'd be hospitalized afterwards!"

Franny laughs.

It's hard to believe that after the ninth grade at Barrow, most of us are leaving. Some of us are applying to public schools; some, like Franny, to private schools.

It's scary. Applying is scary. And the thought of being rejected is worse than scary.

Since I have to leave Barrow, I'd be proud to go to the Bronx High School of Science. I hope I get in.

Now Franny reverses her spoon's direction, circling the fudge and whipped cream counterclockwise, and then digs deep into the chocolate. Slowly, oh so slowly, she brings it up to her mouth and starts to lick the mini sundae on her spoon. Licking this one spoonful alone could take a month. I am now in physical pain from watching her, so I gobble down three enormous spoonfuls, take a deep breath, and stop.

Suddenly I hear my name being called. Ronnie and Toby come walking toward us.

"Hi!" says Ronnie. "Did you go shopping this morning? Us too."

She stands for a second, lifting her long black hair in her hands and holding it up to the back of her head.

Toby takes a spoon and scoops up a taste of my sundae.

She swallows it and then starts to reach for another taste.

"Sit down," I say warmly as I gently guide the spoon toward Franny's bowl.

They both slide into our booth.

"Guess what?" Ronnie says. "I saw Doris Kledge. She says that the column is going to be out this week on Thursday and that it's so hot that when she wrote it she had to keep her legs crossed!"

"That's disgusting," Toby says, and then looks at me.

"Guess who's on his way over here, Gil? Shep Newman and Don Melnick. They were picking out tennis shorts at Morris Brothers."

Sure enough, the door opens and in they walk.

Just seeing Shep makes me nervous. I want to stare and stare at him. I can't take my eyes off him sometimes. On the other hand, if he looks at me—I look at my shoes.

Shep is wearing a white tennis shirt that says U.S. OPEN on it. You can see his chest muscles, the two lines that separate his chest from his stomach. It's like male cleavage. He's gorgeous. He also has a halo of curly, dirty-blond hair and big brown eyes . . . and he's already almost six feet tall.

Don is just the opposite. He's short and angular and dark and sexy. He's got a great smile.

As they walk in, Don waves at Franny. And Shep looks right at us and waves.

So does my heart.

Shep waves again and it's almost as though he's waving at me. It couldn't be.

But it is. Because then he calls out, "Hey—Gilly. Just the person I've been looking for!"

Oh, my God. I must be hallucinating.

Franny sticks an elbow in my ribs. "It's that blouse," she whispers. "You look great in that blouse."

Don moves into another booth, winking at Franny.

She gives him a slow wave. She's not really interested in Don.

But Shep is approaching our table, his enormous brown eyes directly on me.

My heart starts pounding. My hands start shaking.

"Hi, Shep," Toby says, sexily.

He nods to her. Even his nod is masculine.

"Hey, Gilly," he says, "I was just wondering . . . uh . . . you're taking the Bronx Science test, aren't you?"

I nod. I'd speak, but my heart is blocking my lips.

"Well . . . a few of us are forming a math study group . . . and we were wondering if you'd like to join us. We're meeting tomorrow night and every Sunday till the test."

"Uh, sure. I'm taking it. Sure."

"Great. So . . . are you interested in joining us?"

Am I interested? If this is the first step to having his children, of course I'm interested.

"Uh . . . I guess so," I say.

"Great." He stares right at my chest. And then back up at my eyes.

"I'm at 501 West End. Just a few blocks from you. Apartment 9G. Could you be there tomorrow night at eight o'clock?"

"Sure."

"Nice shirt."

And he walks over to Don's booth.

Slowly ... oh, so slowly ... as Shep slides into the booth with his back facing us, a grin begins to form on my mouth. I try to stay calm.

Toby helps.

"You sure are good at math," she says.

"I'm telling you," Franny says, ignoring her, "he likes you. He never would have asked you otherwise. He likes you, Gil!" She gives me a hug.

"Who's to say what motivates people?" Toby muses.

Even Ronnie is impressed. "You know, he just made the lacrosse team."

I nod at her.

Does he like me?

I know he liked my blouse.

And the way he looked at me—he might like me. He might.

If he does, it would be the best thing to happen to me ever. Ever.

Shep Newman might like Gilly Miles!

Gilly Miles might get Shep Newman!

What I want to know is—where is Doris Kledge when you need her!

Chapter 11

I'm lying in bed and I can't sleep.

So I stare at three stick-em stars that are stuck on my ceiling since third grade.

Please, God . . . make Shep like me.

My life is so confusing.

But if Shep were interested . . . everything would be different.

And let's face it, God . . . you haven't exactly been bending over backwards on my behalf.

I'm sorry. I'm sorry. I didn't mean that. I know you're doing the best you can.

I didn't mean that either. I mean, you do everything perfectly.

When you want to . . .

Okay, okay . . . so I'm being sarcastic. I can't help it.

It's just that I don't think this is too much to ask. I

know you're busy preventing a nuclear holocaust, but can't you make sure there's world peace *and* make Shep Newman like me?

It would make me so happy.

He's so cute. He's not one of those good-looking but shallow types either. He's popular for a reason. Because he's a great guy. I'll bet he kisses fantastically. I'll bet he makes Arnold's kiss feel like nothing.

Ronnie called before I went to bed. She told me that Shep didn't just ask me for our study group on Sunday. He asked Greg Wing and Scott James. But he didn't ask Sharri Cunningham or Andrea Lapotin. And they're the smartest girls in the class. He must be interested!

He must! All I'm asking of you is to push him a little. It'd take a second.

Okay, if it's a matter of Shep or world peace, work on world peace. Of course.

But if it's a matter of me and Shep vs. anything for Toby Konig, then for crying out loud—use your head!

I didn't mean that. I know you'll do what's best.

I know you will.

I'm sure you have a plan.

I'm just a young person who's going to trust you.

I'm just a young person whose entire happiness is in your hands.

Entire happiness.

Have a nice night.

Chapter 12

_I_t's Sunday morning and four of us are waiting for Victory and her parents to move in. Me. Franny. Arnold. And Arnold's dad.

At 12:10 the service elevator stops at our floor and two moving men and furniture start to come out. First an old sofa covered by a dirty moving pad. Then a piano. Then an old easy chair. An old oak table. Then lots of paintings, all covered by pads.

I'm kind of excited. I look at Franny. She's nervous.

After a few more rounds of moving men coming out of the elevator, Mr. and Mrs. Norton arrive. He's holding some paintings and she's holding a carton. Norman Dorfenberg greets them immediately.

"Hello," he says. "I just wanted to introduce myself and welcome you to our building. I'm Norm Dorfenberg."

They smile. As they chat, the elevator descends.

I know the next trip up will be Victory.

Arnold sits on the fourth step of our staircase. There is a big brown paper bag beside him which he keeps looking at nervously.

Now the elevator rattles back up, the door opens, and Victory emerges. She's carrying an enormous, life-size statue of a nude guy. I think it's Michelangelo's David. It's terrific looking except for one thing. The whole statue is marble white. But she's painted his you-know-what purple.

"Hi!" Victory cries. She runs over to Arnold, gives him a kiss, and then runs back to me and tries to give me a hug. Unfortunately, the you-know-what is sticking in my belly button.

"Sorry . . ." She puts him down. "This is Purple David. I found him on the street. He's kind of my confidant, my male muse. The brother I never had. You like him? . . . I decorated him myself."

I try to stare at David's face and be cool.

"Oh, absolutely. He reminds me of my brother."

Everybody laughs, including Franny. Who becomes hysterical giggling.

Victory looks at her.

Don't giggle, Franny.

"Hi, Victory," she says, now just smiling. "I just wanted to welcome you to the eleventh floor. I hope we can . . . you know . . . be friends."

Victory nods. "Sure. Who are you?"

Franny flinches, but recovers.

"Fran Hodges. I live next to Gilly. I met you at school? Maybe, after you're settled, you might want to

61

come over to my house and the three of us can have some hot chocolate and watch some old *All My Children*s on my VCR."

"You must be kidding." She pauses, retreating. "I'll tell you the truth . . . I've got so much unpacking to do. But . . . thanks. Thanks so much."

"Sure," Franny says. Naturally her feelings are hurt. She eyes me with a significant look, a look which says, "I told you the girl is a bitch."

But Franny should know better. Watching soap operas would never be Victory's thing. They're shallow, they're adolescent, they're drivel. Victory would never like them as much as we do.

I'm kind of bored with them myself.

Now Franny heads for her apartment, not taking her eyes off me.

"I'll see you in a few minutes," I say. I feel bad but I can't leave now. Not yet.

All of a sudden we hear the sound of a throat clearing.

"Eh heh eh heh."

It's Norman Dorfenberg, the CPA. He walks over to Victory and introduces himself. "I've heard a lot about you."

Victory smiles at Mr. Dorfenberg. "Thank you," she says. She almost unconsciously looks him over from head to toe, stopping at several places along the way, and then gives him a big, sexy smile.

"Well . . . ," says Norman nervously. "Uh . . . I can't stay. I promised Mrs. Dorfenberg I'd go over to Zabar's and get some whitefish."

Victory nods warmly. "I understand . . . whitefish goes quickly on Sunday."

Mr. Dorfenberg swallows out loud, the way Arnold sometimes does, and retreats. As he passes Arnold to go down the stairs, he slaps his son on the shoulder, clears his throat, and mutters, "Good luck, son."

As soon as Norman's gone, Victory claps. "Gilly . . . you look great! I'm sorry about your friend, but you understand . . . I don't want to be rude . . . but I'm not the soap type."

I nod.

"As a matter of fact . . . maybe you want to come over this afternoon. Arnold and I are going to start writing the script for the movie."

I hesitate.

"I . . . I'd love to, but . . . I promised Fran."

Victory nods. "Sure . . . no problem. But if you can dump her . . . come on in."

"Gee . . . Victory . . . please don't say that. Franny's great. She's been my friend since I was a little kid."

She shrugs, a little disappointed in me. "Suit yourself."

Meanwhile, Arnold is just standing there, holding something behind his back. Now, with only Victory and me left in the hall, he brings out a paper bag. Bowing slightly, he pulls out a tablecloth, a bottle of ginger ale, and then—a small jar of caviar!

"I thought a caviar and champagne-ish picnic might be nice to celebrate your arrival. What do you think?" he says.

I think Arnold's voice is changing. It's getting deeper.

Victory is grinning from ear to ear.

"I love it!" she says.

"I thought you would."

I can't believe Arnold thought of this.

He turns to me. "Gil . . . would you like to join us?"

Victory nods in agreement. "Please, Gil. You have to at least be at my welcome party."

"Well," I say. "Sure. If I'm not in the way."

"Not at all," says Arnold. "But could you do me a little favor? Could you bring out some crackers and a knife? And maybe some napkins?"

I look at Arnold, a little annoyed. But I say, "All right."

"Great," he says. "And listen, while you're in there—if you happen to have any chopped onion or cream cheese . . . that's how my dad makes it . . . it's delicious."

I give him a deadly stare.

"Eh . . . forget it. It's not important. Just hurry back. Okay?"

I nod. The steam is starting to reach my ears again. But I just say, "Onions? No problem."

As I leave, I see Arnold spreading a tablecloth on the hallway floor; he even puts out a little candlestick with a long, tapered candle. I can't believe it. My Arnold. My nerdy Arnold being so romantic.

As I reach into my hall bureau drawer, I can see them out of the corner of my eye. Victory walks over to stand behind him. She kisses him on the neck. Arnold turns around and puts his arms around her and kisses her back. I know their mouths are open.

I pass my mom. She's on the phone with her brother, my Uncle Billy, from California. He's a film producer. She's trying to talk and peek out the door at us at the same time.

"Sorry, Billy," she says. "Neighbors just moving in."

My Uncle Billy and she are real close. My mom says she fought with him growing up even more than I fight with Jeff. Now she's real proud of him.

He's so successful that he wears jewelry everywhere.

Victory would hate him.

Jeff comes out of the bathroom and passes the open door. He stares too.

"Is that Arnold?" he asks incredulously.

I nod.

"And that's Victory?"

I nod again.

"No wonder he dumped you!"

"He didn't dump me!" I say angrily. "We're friends! I dumped him . . . years ago."

"Right . . ."

And Jeff walks into the kitchen.

We are friends, Arnold and I.

I mean what *do* I care if he likes Victory? I'm happy for Arnold. I really am. I'm happy for both of them.

Happy. Happy. Happy.

It's Shep Newman I want.

Holding the napkins and crackers, I follow Jeff into the kitchen, open the refrigerator door, and scan the shelves for an onion.

Then I close the door.

On the other hand . . . let them get their own onions.

Naturally, after the picnic, when I go in to speak to Franny, she's very upset.

I can't blame her.

Victory was pretty rude.

But also honest.

I never say what I really think like that. Or at least not enough.

"The girl is obnoxious, Gil!" Franny shouts at me, shaking her fists. "Can't you see that?"

"Yeah. I can."

But she's great too, I think. And she wants to make a movie with *me* as a star. Sure, it'll make me throw up with fear, but it's so exciting.

I don't say any of that, of course.

I just say, "She's definitely not nice. Definitely not. So . . . you want to play 'Who Shall I Marry?' or maybe watch the soaps?"

Franny shrugs. But she agrees and takes the cards out of her night table.

As she shuffles them, she looks up at me.

"I'll tell you the truth, Gil. If you're friendly with her, it's not going to be so easy to be friendly with me."

"I know, Franny. I know."

I look at Franny's face. She doesn't just look angry. She looks sad.

"I know what Victory thinks of me," she says. "She just thinks I'm conventional. Middle class. I know her type. Well, she's wrong! I'm a person too!"

"I know that, Fran. I think you're great."

Strange. I should feel bad that Franny feels insecure. But somehow, it's making me feel more secure.

Is that disgusting?

I change the subject to wipe the feeling from my mind.

"I'm going to Shep's tonight for the study group."

"Right!" And she adds, but without much enthusiasm: "That's great, Gil. Promise to stop in when you come back? I want to hear what happens."

I promise.

Even though I just promised Victory the same thing.

Chapter 13

_S_tanding in front of Shep's door, I try to calm down. I take a deep breath, put a smile on my face, take an even deeper breath, smile even wider, and toss my scarf over my shoulder, Franny style. Then I ring.

And wait.

Finally the door opens. It's Scott.

Scott is 180 pounds, five foot ten, and is on the Barrow soccer team. He's a nice guy, I've known him since kindergarten, but we've never been able to talk to each other.

"Hey," he says, then turns right back around and walks away. I follow him, and as we reach the living room, Shep appears, walking toward me. He's grinning.

"Great! Gil, I'm glad you're here. We're ready to start."

He helps me off with my coat. As he touches my shoulder, my heart is pounding with nervousness. He gently removes my coat, tosses it on the couch, but it just as gently slips to the floor. We ignore it.

I follow him into the dining room. Seated around the large glass table are Greg Wing, Scott . . .

And two girls!

One of them is Tamara Apthorp, who I walk to school with, the dark beauty who goes to Dalton. Greg Wing has his knuckly hand on hers.

The other girl I don't know.

"Hi, Tamara!" I say, real glad to see her. In this group she's practically my best friend.

She waves. "Hi, Gil!"

"I didn't know you wanted to go to Science," I say.

What I really mean is, why would someone as rich as you want to go to a public school?

Shep introduces the other girl. "And this is Amanda Apple. She goes to Calhoun. Amanda—this is Gilly Miles. Now—let's get to it."

Shep sits down. Amanda sits beside him. To his left is another empty chair. That one's for me.

As soon as I sit, I try to unobtrusively lean my chair back, behind Shep, and get a good look at Amanda. Who is she? She couldn't be Shep's new girlfriend, could she?

She's not that much prettier than me. She's got a sweet smile, and long black hair down to her waist. The hair is gorgeous.

Maybe she's Scott's girlfriend.

Shep passes out Xerox sheets to everybody.

"These are the sheets from the private tutoring

course that Mr. Greenstein teaches. Andrea Lapotin is taking the course. She gave it to me."

Ah-ha. That's why Andrea's not here.

Greg gets up. "Okay. If you want to start—read the first page. It explains factoring. And it's easy. Missy taught it to us real well."

Missy's our math teacher.

"Review it," he continues, "and then we'll do the questions on the next page together."

Scanning the sheet, I can see that Greg's right. It *is* easy.

Amanda gets up, stroking her long hair with her hand and looking at the group. "Maybe everybody'd like some popcorn?"

There are immediately cries of "great idea," "sure," etc. And Amanda picks up her study sheet and heads for the kitchen.

She knows exactly where it is.

Maybe she's a relative of Shep's.

She can't be his girlfriend.

She can't be.

Look, God, if she's his girlfriend, then you and I are through. I don't mean through. But why get me over here . . . if you're just going to disappoint me?

"Okay, Gil . . . do you think you understand the fundamentals?"

"Huh? Oh . . . yeah . . . definitely. I know factoring pretty well. Let's go to the questions."

Each of us begins to work on the practice test sheet.

They're easy. I finish first, and touch Shep's shirt.

"Maybe I'll go in and help Amanda . . . she's missing this and I'm finished," I say.

70

Shep laughs. "Amanda's not taking the test. She's just a friend. She lives next door to me."

God . . . you can't do this to me.

"Yeah." Scott grins. "I invited her."

I never doubted you, God. Never. Honest.

Amanda comes in with the popcorn. When you think about it, she is kind of pretty. . . .

"Oh my gosh," she says. "I forgot the salt."

I volunteer to get it.

And as I start into the kitchen, I feel the presence of a body following me.

I glance around nervously.

It's not Amanda. It's Shep.

"We also need napkins. And you don't know where the salt is."

I nod.

As he walks behind me, I know he is staring at the back of my body.

I stand taller as I walk. I wonder if I put my belt through all the belt loops in the back.

My heart is pounding.

We enter the kitchen. He reaches for the napkins in a cabinet. I walk to the far end of the kitchen, where the table is, and get the salt shaker. We meet in the middle, near the door, ready to walk back.

In my mind, we both stop at the butcher block. And he says, "Wait, Gil. Wait." And my heart is pounding. And he puts his arms around my neck and says, "It's more than salt that I want." And in my mind I'm saying, "Yes, I know, Shep, yes, I want more than salt too, yes." And in my mind, he lifts up my chin and he kisses me, wetly but gently. I'm his.

But in real life we bump into each other near the butcher block and he says, "'scuse me," and he grins. And I grin. True, I grin for as long as possible, and I look in his eyes, trying to say, without actually saying anything, "I'm crazy about you." I make my eyes as passionate as possible. But nothing. Absolutely no response.

I follow him out to the dining room, where he says . . .

"Tadaaa . . . popcorn . . . hot and salty. Come and get it."

Damn. I was alone with him. That was my big chance.

Okay. Maybe I only stared and smiled for two seconds. It felt like a year.

I mean, I'm not a flirt. What can I do? Be what I'm not?

I sit back down in my seat. He smiles at me again. I smile back.

"Put out your hands, Gil," he says. I do. And he fills them with popcorn.

Chapter 14

I'm standing in my hallway. It's almost ten o'clock. Nothing else happened.

Well, not nothing. Shep complimented my earrings. Which were actually Franny's.

I knock on Franny's door.

She peeks out the peephole, then opens the door.

"How'd it go?"

I shake my head. "Nothing. Nada. Rien. Zippo. I'm not dead. I'm not alive. There may have been some microscopic developments that I'm not aware of."

"You want to come in?"

I shake my head again. "I'm going to sleep."

"It's still not out of the question, Gil. These things take time. I spoke to Don Melnick tonight and I asked him."

"What'd he say?"

"He said he didn't know either. But . . . you can't give up. Shep's a real winner."

"I know. And I've made a tremendous advance. He knows I'm alive. He's seen me breathe. Good night, Fran."

"Good night, Gil."

As soon as her door shuts, I tiptoe over to Victory's apartment and knock softly.

She peeks her head out.

"Hi. I thought you weren't coming . . ."

"Can I come in?" I whisper.

"Sure. I'll make some hot chocolate."

Hot chocolate. Victory makes hot chocolate? I would have thought she made ginseng tea or something.

I walk into the apartment, past the hall, and into the kitchen. I sit down.

It's so strange to see Mrs. Hearn's apartment furnished with different furniture. Instead of the old Formica table I used to sit at so much, my elbows are resting on a glass table. Instead of all the mahogany furniture and knickknacks, there's butcher block and modern art.

It's nice, but . . . nothing is left of Mrs. Hearn.

"So," Victory says, pouring some milk into a saucepan for me, "now where did you go? To see some guy Arnold says you've been crazy about forever?"

"Yeah. His name's Shep and he's great and he asked me to study for the Bronx Science admissions test with a bunch of people. That's why I couldn't come by before. But . . . he didn't seem too interested. It's hopeless. I can tell he doesn't like me, or he'd do something."

"Really? What have you ever done to show him you like him?"

"Huh? Me? I . . . I smile at him. Very warmly."

Victory searches through a big carton till she finds the hot chocolate. She looks up.

"Have you ever told him you've had a crush on him since kindergarten?"

I look at Victory. She's great but she talks like she's from outer space.

"Victory . . . I mean . . . I can't do that sort of thing."

"Sure you can, Gil. I know you. Inside, you're just like me. You hate the rules. The conventions. The hypocrisy. The politeness. Am I right?"

I think of my father and Abigail. "Well . . . yeah."

"Look, it takes courage to say what you feel. I wasn't born this way. I was brought up to be nice . . . a nice girl . . . I don't mean about sex . . . I mean about civilization. And it's bad. You got to get in there and say what you feel. And not be sweet. And timid. You've got to squeeze everything out of life that you can."

Wow.

But all I say is, "It's not easy to say what you feel, Victory. Like . . . what if I told him I liked him but then he didn't like me?"

"So. . . ?"

"So what if he told everybody I said that? Everybody would laugh at me."

"So?" She takes out two mugs from another carton and then pours in the hot-chocolate powder. "So what?

Anyway, maybe they'd even envy you. Because if you did it, then you'd have done what you had to do, you wouldn't waste any more time on Shep, and you could find somebody else."

"You make it sound so simple, Victory."

"I didn't say it was simple. I said it takes courage."

She pours in the milk, plops the cup on the table in front of me, and offers me some carob cookies.

I wonder if carob cookies give you courage.

I don't care. I hate carob cookies.

Victory sits down with her hot chocolate.

"Look, I'll tell you right now, making this movie is going to take some courage. But it'll be good for you. A good way to practice. The first thing you have to do is be a dancer. You're playing my younger self and I dreamt of being a dancer when I was little."

"Gee . . . I . . . I don't know."

"You don't have to be good, you just have to show that you dream of being a dancer. I'll help you, Gil. You know, last year I won third prize in the Young Filmmakers contest at the Whitney. For under fifteens. And this year I want to come in first. You'll be my co-star and associate producer."

I'm fainting. My Uncle Billy, the Hollywood producer, would even be impressed.

She sips her hot chocolate.

"Tell me something, Gil. If you could say anything to anybody, what would it be?"

I want to say, "What is this, the Barbara Walters show?" But I don't. She probably never heard of Barbara Walters.

"Well . . . I guess I'd tell my father's girlfriend . . . just what I think of her. She's such a self-centered princess. She's so mean to me and my mom. I hate her."

"What would happen if you told her?"

"Nothing. She'd scream and cry, and my father would take her side. Then, later, he'd call and take my side, and sound so hurt. Anyway, I decided I'm never spending time with them again."

"See? That's what I mean. You're carrying all that around by yourself. And she's not getting any of it. She's getting off real easy. Smart, isn't she?"

"Well . . . I don't want to see them and make a scene again. Besides, this way I punish my dad. He misses me a lot. This way, I'm . . ." As I talk, it's the first time I understand exactly what I've been doing. "This way, I'm torturing my father. For my mother. Because she won't do it."

And I start to laugh.

Because it sounds ridiculous.

Me. Nice Gilly Miles. Trying to torture my own father.

"Hmm . . ." Victory says sarcastically. "That's not nice. Tsk tsk tsk."

"I know."

And we both start to laugh.

I feel proud.

Imagine me: not nice.

When I stop laughing, I say, "Listen, I gotta go. I hate to be nice, but my mom'll worry. And she deserves someone to be nice to her."

Victory doesn't say anything. She doesn't even nod.

I shrug.

"Say, Victory, where did you decide to go to school? 'Cause maybe you want to walk to school with everybody? There are eleven of us who go to school every morning."

"Sure. When I go, anyway. I decided to try Amsterdam Prep."

"Great."

I say that to be polite. Amsterdam Prep is an alternative public high school where you work three days a week and go to classes two days a week. It's a place for kids who can't fit in any place else, or the last stop for the hoodiest hoods and the druggiest druggies.

"See you tomorrow," she says.

And I slip out her door. Quietly.

Victory is so interesting. So bright. So different. So mature. How could she not be my friend?

I tiptoe across the hall again.

That's when I hear Franny's latch lock. And the peephole slam shut.

Chapter 15

*O*n *my mom's bookshelf, she has this paperback* called *The Lonely Crowd.*

I always wondered what that meant until today.

This morning, Franny didn't pick me up. I overslept and had to get dressed in twenty-six seconds. I forgot to put on socks. I was freezing all day.

On the stoop, everybody was milling around, and Franny wouldn't even look at me. Neither did Toby or Ronnie. Then, just as Tamara, the last girl to arrive, joined us, Victory walked out of our building and I introduced her to everybody.

Doris was the friendliest. She said, "Nice to meet you. I've written a lot about you already."

And Victory said something like, "I know—and you write well, too. It's too bad you can't turn your imagination to some sort of true or worthwhile project, but you have a brilliant mind." Doris was proud as a peacock.

She said, "Wait'll you see Thursday's edition. You and Arnold are my lead. But my second story is new. It's called 'The Feud That Shook West End Avenue.'"

And she gives me and Franny a significant look.

There was deadly silence.

Victory just laughed.

She waved to Franny and said in a real friendly voice, "How were your soaps?"

Franny's voice was colder than a Frozfruit bar.

"Marvelous," she said. "And how was your unpacking? Stimulating and artistic, hmm?"

When we started walking, I didn't know where to stand.

Franny and Toby kept whispering to each other, ignoring me.

The Belson twins, Doris Kledge, Tamara, and Ronnie were all together.

Victory and I were in the back, alone. Then, at the first corner, Victory left, since Amsterdam Prep is in a totally different direction from the rest of our schools.

As soon as Victory was out of sight, Toby muttered, "She's going to Amsterdam Prep? What does she have—a prison record?"

It was awful. It was so tense that Ronnie started to hum "The Star-Spangled Banner."

I tried to talk to Franny. I moved up as close to her as I could get. But she kept walking ahead of me. Finally she turned around and said, "You . . . are a worm turd."

What could I say? I told her there'd been a misunderstanding.

She didn't buy it. "That witch has put me down, and made me feel like dirt . . . and you didn't give a damn. You ignored me completely . . . when you knew how bad I was feeling. And then, after the study session . . ." She just shook her head in disgust.

She was right, but I tried to defend myself. "It's not like that," I said. "Victory opened her door just as I was saying goodbye to you. I was about to go to bed, but she invited me in. . . . I just wanted to be polite, that's all. For Godsakes, I swear . . . what could I do?"

I lied through my teeth but it didn't help.

Toby looked at me like I was a mass murderer and said, "That girl is obnoxious. I hate obnoxious people."

Nothing helped.

I finally got to stand next to Franny. I tilted my head, tried to look like a sad puppy dog, and apologized again.

All she said was, "I warned you, Gil. You really hurt me. And you'll be sorry."

She moved away, next to Ronnie, and I wound up standing with a tilted head, looking like a puppy dog into Toby's eyes.

Yuk.

The rest of the way to Barrow, Ronnie, Toby, and Franny walked together, chatting, and I followed them silently, feeling lousy.

That was my morning.

And school was no better.

One good thing happened. Shep said hello to me in math.

But in the middle of French, which I take with

Franny, just as I thought that maybe she was getting over it, Josh Ferguson came over and said he'd love to come to her party Saturday! He heard it was going to be a big blast.

I was in shock. The tears started to roll down my face. Franny was embarrassed, but gave me a "you deserve it" look.

I wanted to hit her, I really did.

I mean, what did I do that was so terrible?

I made a new friend, that's all.

At lunch, I walked around the block because I knew I wouldn't be invited to join them. In my mind, I kept rehearsing speeches to tell all of them what I felt. But at three o'clock, when I saw Jessica Parrington, Josh, Ronnie, and Franny standing in front of the building, I couldn't do it.

I hid in the Lost and Found until they were gone and then walked home alone.

And now . . .

Now I'm sitting at Teacher's Restaurant, having dinner with my mom and Jeff.

At five o'clock my mom called and told me to meet them here.

So I did.

And I can't believe it. I just can't believe it.

This news makes my fight with Franny back-page news.

Over the chicken gai yung, my mom told us that Uncle Billy offered her a job in California. A chance to work for three months as a production assistant on a movie. She says she hasn't done it for twenty years, but she wants to try it again. It's an opportunity for her to get back the skills she once had, and make some decent money. And since Jeff and I are in the middle of the schoolyear, she's asked my father and Abigail to move into our apartment until she comes back in July.

I'm just sitting in the booth, stunned.

"You can't mean that!" I screech in a whisper.

"Yes, I do, Gilly. Your dad is the only one who can take care of the two of you. I knew you wouldn't want to move downtown to SoHo since it'd be a pain in the neck to get to school. Besides, I think you'll get along better with Abigail if you're on your own turf."

"Mom, how can you do this to me? I hate them."

"Don't talk that way about your father. Look, honey, I'm not happy about it. But I used to love that work. And with the experience, I can come back and get work in New York. I thought of taking you with me, but . . . you graduate from Barrow this year. You have the Bronx Science test. You wouldn't want to leave now, would you?"

I shake my head.

She puts her hands on my shoulders across the table.

"What else can I do?" she says.

Why do parents say "What else can I do?" after they make the mess in the first place by getting divorced and ruining their kids' lives?

"It stinks!" I cry. "It stinks, Mom, and you know it."
She just nods.

"I'll speak to Abigail," she says. "I'll have lunch with her and talk about how you feel. You know, I'm not crazy about her either, but I find a way to be polite."

"You hate her guts, Ma!"

"Well, I . . . I do dislike her . . . uh, intensely . . . but I manage to talk to her and be with her when I have to. And you can, too. And I promise I'll call you as much as I can."

"Every night?"

"Every night. You can handle this, Gilly. You're too nice a kid to make things worse."

Too nice a kid.

Too nice!

Damn it! I'm not!

I've had it with nice.

This is the last straw.

Chapter 16

*W*hen we come home from dinner, at around eight o'clock, I am so upset that I immediately knock on Victory's door.

Her mom answers.

"Hi. I'm Gilly. Is Victory there?"

Her mother shakes her head. "She's at her dad's studio, Gilly. He's using her in a painting."

Victory's father is an artist, like her.

It must be nice to have a parent who's like you.

Damn. I need to talk to somebody.

On the way back to my apartment, I consider ringing Franny's door. But I don't.

Frankly I'm too angry. Franny thinks I betrayed her. But here I have the biggest problem of my life and I can't talk to her.

Wait'll she finds out how miserable I am. And that I didn't tell her. Will she be insulted!

Who can I talk to? I'm all alone.

Here I have two terrific friends. Supposedly. And where are either of them when I need them?

I'm desperate to talk to somebody. Anybody.

So I slouch up the stairs and ring Arnold Dorfenberg's bell.

Mrs. Dorfenberg opens the door.

"Hi, Gilly." She looks at my openly miserable face. "Something wrong?"

"Uh . . . I was wondering if Arnold is around."

"Sure." And she turns and shouts, "Arnold? Arn? Gilly's here! Are you decent?"

In a second, Arnold emerges from his room and walks down the hall toward me. He is not wearing a shirt and he is holding weights in both hands.

He has a nice body.

"Hi, Gil. How ya doin?"

"Swell, Arnold. Can I talk to you?"

"Sure. Come on." And he gestures for me to follow him back to his room. As I do, he makes a muscle with his left bicep. Or tricep or whatever.

"Pretty good, eh, Gil?" he says, not turning around.

I don't say anything.

As we pass the kitchen, Arnold makes a detour toward the refrigerator. "Want some Squirt?"

I shake my head.

Now, as he takes out a cold can, he looks at me carefully.

"Hey . . . Gil . . . what's wrong? You look like you're going to cry."

And when he says it, I just can't help myself.

I burst into tears.

And sob.

Loud, embarrassing sobs.

Mrs. Dorfenberg is standing in the corner of the hall, staring at me. I see Arnold gesture with his eyes for her to stay away. "C'mon," he says. And I follow him into his room.

And tell him the whole story. How Fran won't speak to me just because I've become friendly with Victory. How my mom's abandoning me. How my brother Jeff doesn't understand. How much I hate Abigail. How angry I am at my dad. How I can't handle it. How I can't handle anything. And at the end, I just cry out, "I feel so lonely, I feel so lonely."

Arnold just sits there, looking at me.

I sort of run out of sobs. Sputtering to a stop, I look at him, expecting him to say something wise. Give me some advice. Comfort me.

But he just keeps staring.

"Shee . . . phew . . . that's lousy, Gil," is all he says. And then, "Ya sure you don't want a can of Squirt?"

I shake my head. Now I feel a little less sad and angry. Now I just feel like a total jerk.

We sit there for a while, silently.

"Well . . . I gotta go," I say.

"Yeah. I'll walk you to the door."

"Thanks, Arnold."

"Aw . . . it was nothing."

At the door he says to me, "I'm glad you came and talked to me. I really am. You know what? You look very pretty with your cheeks all flushed like that."

"Thanks, Arnold . . ."

He nods. "Gil . . ." He thinks. Then he says, "Time is the best healer," and he gently closes his door.

I don't know what the hell he's talking about, but when I get back downstairs, to my apartment, I go right in the bathroom and look at my tear-reddened face.

Two seconds later, the phone rings. It's Arnold.

"You know what I wanted to say, Gil. But I didn't."

"What, Arnold?"

"I used to be lonely, too. But things can get a lot better. They're getting better for me. And they will for you. Nothing's as bad as it seems. I think we should start shooting the movie Saturday night when Franny has her party. What do you think?"

"Yeah . . . maybe."

"Maybe definitely. Now don't worry. Remember— you've got me and Victory. You're moving up."

"Thanks, Arnold."

"That's okay. Remember, when the going gets tough, the tough get going."

"Thanks, Arnold."

"It's always darkest before the dawn."

"Thanks, Arnold."

"I'm sorry I couldn't think of this stuff when you were here."

"It's okay, Arnold. Really, it's okay."

"Really?"

"Really."

"Good. Whew. I feel much better. Thanks, Gilly."

"Forget it, Arnold."

Chapter 17

oday's Thursday and I'm waiting for Victory to pick me up as soon as she gets home from school.

For the last three mornings she and I have met at the stoop and walked one block together. Then I continue on alone.

Starting next week Victory will go to school on Monday and Thursday only. The rest of the week she's working at a film-editing studio. So I'll be completely on my own in the morning.

Victory said I could move in with her when my dad and Abigail come. But that would be a little ridiculous. I could just see me standing at the elevator: Out would walk Franny, who I'm not speaking to . . . And then, out would walk my father and Airhead, who wouldn't speak to me.

Anyway, I've been thinking about what Victory said.

It's time for a change. It's time to take some chances.

Like today's our first day of shooting. I'm scared . . . but I'm going to do it.

Actually, I have no choice. I made excuses Tuesday and Wednesday afternoon. So today's the day.

This morning Doris Kledge's *West End Avenue Winds* came out. The lead item, about Victory and Arnold, was pretty hot.

Who'd have thought the first boy on our block to lose his . . . baby fat . . . would be Arnold Dorfenberg. He's a lucky guy, now that he's the paramour of our controversial new neighbor, Victory Norton, talented moviemaker and wearer of the tightest pants on the West Side.

I'm sure Arnold isn't sleeping with Victory. He wouldn't know how. I hope his mother doesn't read this tonight. She'll have a cow.

Then there was an item about Toby going out with a boy from Bucknell—which I am sure Toby is totally making up. And then there was the item about me and Franny. It was pretty serious. It said:

This reporter is sad today. The oldest friendship on our block has turned into a feud. We're not sure what caused it, but whatever it is, this reporter hopes they get back together, and we're all walking the streets of New York side by side again.

Wednesday, Ronnie came up to me during gym and said she still wanted to be friends, but that right now she thought Fran needed her more, since I had Victory as a friend and I was making the movie.

Everyone's jealous of this movie. It sounds great to be in a movie. But it's not so easy. Like today, I'm supposed to wear a tight white leotard and white slinky skirt and float around between the columns at the old boat-basin rotunda near the Hudson River. Victory told me I have to act dreamy, graceful, and sexy.

Me act dreamy, graceful, and sexy? That's ridiculous. She's probably going to give up in five minutes. And then I won't have the movie, I won't have a new friend, and I won't have any old friends.

The doorbell rings. I answer it. It's Victory.

"Hi! Are you ready?" She's carrying the costume.

"I . . . I don't feel that well . . . honestly."

"I understand." She hands me a bag. "Put this on and let's go. The light should be just right by the river today."

"Right."

My first decision is whether I should get dressed in front of Victory.

"I'll be right out," I say. I decide to go into the bathroom instead.

As I put on the white top and long white dancing skirt, I flirt with myself in the mirror. This outfit is sexy. Very sexy.

As soon as I walk out, Victory whistles. I rush for the closet, where I cover myself with a yellow slicker.

"That's perfect, Gil. It's very modern dancer, very Isadora Duncan."

"Who's that?"

"Just one of the most beautiful, exotic, romantic, adventurous dancers that ever lived. When I was younger I wanted to be just like her. And you look great . . . I mean grrreat in that outfit! If I were you I'd just run to the river in that dress. And not hide it."

"Victory . . . one step at a time. I'm scared to death. I can't believe I'm doing this at all. And I'd rather throw up on my yellow slicker than Whatshername Duncan's dress."

She laughs. "Sorry. You're right. I don't want to be pushy. I know you're scared, but I want you to know I'm grateful. And I do know you'll be terrific."

"Thanks."

"I'm proud of you."

"Thanks."

"Let's go."

"I can't."

Victory takes my hand, and pushes me in front of her, and we head for the elevator.

I hate her. She's maneuvered me into this. I hate her.

Outside our building, she takes my elbow again and steers us to the boat basin. I try to take a big breath. I feel every rib in my body.

"Beautiful . . . beautiful day!" Victory says.

"Eh . . ." I shrug.

Actually, it is a beautiful day. And it's particularly pretty by the Hudson River. A lot of people outside New York City don't realize we live right by water, and see sunsets every night, and can walk and fish and jog right by the river—just a block away from us. It's not exactly like the country, but it's very pretty. People don't realize that New York isn't just tall buildings and weirdos. It's got that too . . . but it's got a whole lot more.

As we walk toward the Hudson, Victory talks to me.

"Gilly, do you hate me?"

I nod.

"Good. That's okay. You feel a lot of things before you act. Mostly vulnerable. And that's good."

I try to say "good," but the words don't come out. Even as I walk, my knees feel like rubber.

"The key to good acting, Gilly, is privacy. And concentration. That's why I didn't ask Arnold along this first time. If you can get to a state where you are inside your head, pretending . . . like you did when you were a kid . . . you won't notice anybody. Acting is private. That's why so many shy people can do it."

I look at her. Victory always says something interesting.

"When we get down there"—she steers me down some steps and we can now see the river—"I want you to forget everything but what you're feeling. Today, you are me . . . a young girl who dreams of being a dancer."

"Right."

"You're free . . . carefree and full of fantasies. You'll be doing leaps and graceful slides . . . glissades, they're called . . . but I just want you to improvise them . . . running to a column, curtsying, dipping, picking up the hem of your dress, leaning against the marble, your hands clasped behind you . . . total fantasy. Okay?"

She's nuts. There's no way totally timid me can leap around the Hudson River. No way.

We reach the 79th Street boat basin. That's a small dock where some sailboats and yachts are moored, but mostly where a bunch of houseboats are permanently anchored. Right before the basin are steps that lead to a rotunda with columns. And in the center there's a huge round fountain which hasn't worked for years.

Thank goodness. Nobody's there. Nobody will watch. Of course we could be murdered, but at least I won't be embarrassed.

Victory, who's been carrying a small camera case, puts it down and starts to take some film and a camera out.

"Victory, I . . . I want to do this, I really do, but . . ."

"Okay, Gil, I'll tell you what . . . which of the things I mentioned scares you the least?"

"Uh . . . I don't know. Let me think."

Who can think? I'm so nervous . . .

"How about if today all I ask you to do is lean against one of the columns and look a little . . . tiny bit . . . dreamy? How's that? You just lean . . . and look up at the sky. Can you do that?"

"Uh . . . maybe."

"Great."

Victory puts the camera to her shoulder and walks me to the least graffiti'ed Roman column. She practically moves me, like a mannequin, until my back is leaning against it.

"Lift your head up. Good. Now think . . . think of a beautiful Greek lover far far away . . . over the sea beyond."

She gestures to the Hudson.

Beyond the Hudson is no Greek lover. Beyond the Hudson is New Jersey.

"Come on, now. Picture him. He's gorgeous. He's sensitive, he's everything you ever wanted. By the way, you look so beautiful . . . so serene. . . . Now . . . think of that lover . . . that winsome, handsome, sensitive Greek boy with long, elegant fingers. . . ."

Hmmm . . . he sounds great.

"Can you see him, Gil? Now raise your chin. Look up, past the river. Close your eyes and raise your head."

I lift my head. I close my eyes. I try to concentrate on the Greek boy. He's beautiful . . . he looks like a living version of Victory's David.

I try to envision it.

"You loved each other, but he's been called away. To war against the vicious Turks. He was so young. So handsome. Can you remember his last kiss? Can you remember it? Try to remember it, Gil."

I remember. I remember. It was wonderful.

"But now a messenger arrives. You turn to face him as he approaches you. His head is down as he delivers the news. Your lover, your gentle lover, Alexis, has died at the hands of the Turks. Oh, my God. Your love . . . gone forever. Forever, Gil . . . And you're carrying his child. . . ."

My jaw drops. I really feel terrible. One minute I'm in love with a Greek god. The next minute I'm a pregnant widow. Love snatched from me again. I look out at the sea, mourning my loss. Poor me.

And I hear the camera motor running.

And then Victory's voice. "Gilly . . . you were born to act. Great. It's great."

And I lift my head higher, I take another mournful breath, and I look at the sky, and the vast universe in front of me that has taken away my Greek boyfriend. I'm devastated . . . in a poetic sort of way.

"That's a take!" Victory says.

I smile. I love movie words like "take."

"That wasn't so hard," I say.

"Of course not, Gil . . . you're good. Would I waste film on you if I thought you weren't?"

It made sense.

"Thanks. Are we through?"

Victory winks at me and lifts the camera to her shoulder again. "Almost. Almost. Just one more time. And this time could you take off the yellow slicker?"

She grins. We both burst out laughing.

"Could you do that?"

I nod. Because I feel terrific. I love acting. I *love* it.

"Hey . . ." I smile, snapping open the slicker and tossing it over to her. "No problem, Victory. No problem."

Chapter 18

*A*s we walk back to the building, I spot Franny coming in the opposite direction. She's walking with Toby.

I look down as we walk, trying not to make any eye contact with them.

"Saturday's going to be a little more challenging, Gil," Victory says. "We're going to work on the Lower East Side. And Arnold will come too. Okay?"

I know Fran has seen me. I grin warmly at Victory. "Sure." I laugh loudly. "I'd love it. That will be faabulous fun."

Victory looks at me like I'm crazy. I look back at her, intently.

"Can I take a look at the camera, Victory? I just want to see how it feels. Okay?"

I know if I'm holding the camera it'll drive Franny crazy with jealousy.

Victory zips open the camera bag, holds up a lens, looking for the camera. I just grab the lens. It'll do. I start inspecting it super carefully as we walk into the lobby. Out of the corner of my eye I see that Franny has also entered the lobby.

We're waiting for the elevator when the two of them reach us.

We nod to each other.

They're both wearing great earrings. The same great earrings. They've obviously just gone shopping together.

And Franny is wearing a boy's sports ring around her neck. I wonder why.

I try not to stare at Franny's neck. Instead I start up a phony conversation with Victory.

"Boy, this is some lens. Wouldn't it be something if we won an award? Like you did last year. Were you in *The New York Times* last year, Victory?"

Victory smiles at Franny and then says to me, "We could win an award. You're such a good actress."

Franny and Toby stare at the dial that indicates what floor the elevator is on.

"Like right now," Victory continues. "You're acting like crazy."

Franny and Toby look at each other and smirk.

Why can't Victory be a phony for five minutes, just to impress my ex-friend? I mean, why does she have to be so direct and honest? Franny would have done it, I know that.

"How are you, Fran?" Victory asks.

"Fine, thank you. And yourself?"

"Fine, thank you. And Gilly's fine too. It looks like we're all fine."

Now Franny looks Victory in the eye. Her eyes are daggers. I know she wants to say something devastating but nothing comes out. So she turns to me. Still, nothing comes out. And I can see that for a second there's more hurt in her eyes than anger.

The elevator arrives, the door opens, and the four of us walk in, turn around, and stand silently, staring at the metal elevator gate, not daring to look at each other.

When we reach the eleventh floor, they get out first, and I glance quickly at the shopping bag that Toby is carrying. Party plates and plastic cups and paper decorations. For Saturday night's party. To which I am not invited.

It makes me feel bad. But it also makes me mad.

I've just had a great time starting the film with Victory. What did I ever do with Franny, anyway, but watch soaps and talk about boys and go shopping? I mean, how can you compare Victory and Franny? You can't.

Goodbye and good riddance, Franny Hodges.

My loss is your gain.

I mean your loss is my gain.

I mean, goodbye and good luck.

Who needs you?

Chapter 19

*A*s I walk into the apartment, I'm still so mad that I slam the door and practically run over my mother, who's about to walk out.

"What's the matter?" she says, staring at me.

"Matter? Nothing's the matter. Why should something be the matter?"

"You look angry, that's why. So how'd the filming go?"

"Ma . . . it was so so so great. I mean, I can't believe how great it was. I acted for the first time in my life . . . and it was great."

"Well, you acted once before. Remember? You played the scribe in some old Gilbert and Sullivan play."

"Eww . . . ohh . . . yuk." I remember it very well. I was nine years old, and all I had to do was step forward and say, "Yes, sire, it is written" three times.

It was a stupid, tiny part, but I was so scared I almost didn't go to school.

"Well, that's great, Gil. You're going to have a great time." She pauses. "And how's Franny taking all this?"

She knows. She talks to Franny's mom, so I know she knows. I hate when moms try to manipulate you into talking.

"Fine, Ma. She's taking it fine."

"I haven't seen her around lately. . . ."

"Well . . . I've been so busy. . . ."

My mom looks at me and frowns.

"Look, Mother, if you're so interested in my life, you might try living with me till I'm grown." And I walk into my room.

I'm not taking crap from anybody anymore.

Not me. Not Gilly Miles, the actress.

I drop the slicker to the floor, take off my white skirt and leotard, and reach for my dungarees.

Before I do, I look at myself in the mirror.

I do have a kind of long and dancerish figure. Not like Ronnie, but not bad. I could grow a little on top— that would be good news. But maybe I'm not just skinny; maybe I'm shaped like the great Isadora Duncan. Of course, my face is really dull. Dull dull dull. But, when I lower my jaw and suck in my cheeks . . . it isn't that bad. If I lost ten pounds I'd actually look that way. Maybe.

There's a knock on the door. My mom.

"Yeah?"

"Can I come in, Gil?" she says.

"Yeah. Sure. If you want." I turn away from the mirror, put on some undies, and am putting on my bra when she walks in and stands by my bed.

"I'm leaving Saturday. This Saturday. Shooting starts Monday and Uncle Billy needs me."

Oh, God. No. Don't let her go. I turn away, and with my back to my mom, stepping into my jeans, I say, "Have a wonderful time. Have a wonderful life. Send Uncle Billy all my love."

She walks toward me. She taps me on the shoulder. I turn around and fall right into a hug.

"I love you very much, Gilly Miles. I'm going to miss you and Jeff a lot. But I also know that you've worried about me too much lately . . . and when I come back, I hope that won't be necessary anymore. Do you understand?"

I nod.

"I know you've been having a tough time these last few days. Franny's mom told me the two of you aren't speaking. I know she's having a party this Saturday."

"I really don't care about that, Mom. I swear. I'm friends with Victory now. And, frankly, Franny was boring me. Plus, I hate her guts."

"Maybe you'll make up when I'm gone. . . ."

"Ma . . . you're not listening to me. I swear . . . our friendship is over. Period."

"Yeah. Right. But three months is a long time. Maybe you'll find out you still have something in common . . . like your whole lives . . . or laughing together . . . or boys . . . or the same values . . . you know. . . ."

"Maaaaa!"

My mom just stands there, staring at me.

Sometimes she does that. She just stands and looks at me. I know she's feeling one of those "where has the time gone, she's gotten so big" feelings.

But all she says is, "I'm going to call every day, just like I said."

"Good."

"I'm about to meet Abigail for dinner, like I promised. I don't want you to feel that just because I'm leaving for three months, you can't depend on me. Or trust me. You can. This is just an emergency. A personal emergency. Like when Grandpa was dying and I had to be in Florida for a month. But I came back. And I'll come back this time."

"I know."

"Do you want me to talk about anything specifically, with Abigail?"

I shake my head. "No. Just send her my regards and tell her I worship the ground she's superficial on."

"Gilly!"

I take a deep breath. "Look, Ma. You're leaving. You're doing what you want to do. Don't ask me to feel what you want me to feel. Because I can't. And I won't. If things work out, swell. If not, well, then not. I'll try. But I'm not trying any harder than she does just because I'm the kid."

My mom looks at me, impressed.

"You can tell her that, too," I add.

She grins. "I think not. But I will tell her that you're going to try. Is that fair to tell her?"

"If she tries, I will."

"Good. Because I'm sure she will."

And I'm sure she won't. The woman can be nice for ten minutes at a time, maximum.

As my mom walks toward the door, she turns to stare at me again.

"You're growing into a terrific young woman, Gilly Miles. You really are."

Usually I'm embarrassed when my mother compliments me. I say, "Aw, Ma," or, "You're just a little partial," or, "I am not." But this time I smile.

"Thanks," I say. Because I'm working on it.

Chapter 20

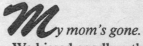y *mom's gone.*

We kissed goodbye this morning and I didn't feel a thing. I didn't cry or anything.

She hugged me and made me promise to have dinner tonight with my father and Abigail and Jeff.

I said yes. But it's getting very late.

I promised, but I can't wait much longer.

About fifteen minutes ago I heard Ronnie and Toby arrive. They must be helping Franny get ready for the party.

God, I don't want to be here. I don't want to see my whole class show up. I don't want to stand at the elevator and have somebody like Jessica Parrington or Josh Ferguson walk out and stare at me.

And feel sorry for me.

Maybe I was a little insensitive to Franny, but I don't deserve this. I don't.

I've got to get out of here.

Even making the movie tonight will be less scary than hanging out here.

I don't even care that Victory says I have to play her as an old lady. In fact, she says I have to wear a beard.

She knows girls don't have beards, but it's symbolic. The child is father of the man. Or woman. She said.

Everything Victory says seems so intellectual, so original, so interesting.

So totally incomprehensible.

Franny would probably call it pretentious junk.

Maybe it is. But I don't care.

Where are my stupid father and Airhead? They're two hours late. It's almost seven o'clock.

I'm starting to get nervous.

I can tell I'm nervous because I'm sitting at the table in front of three napkins that I seem to have shredded into a thousand pieces.

Moo shu napkins.

Get me out of here!

The phone rings.

I pick it up.

"Gil?"

Finally. It's Jeff.

"Jeff," I say. "Where are you? You were supposed to be here hours ago."

"Sorry. But it took a while to pack."

"I'm sure. Two hundred pairs of designer jeans can't

106

be packed in a minute. And ... I can't stay much longer."

"Gillee ... we're late because we had to carry everything down from the fifth floor. The elevator broke. But we'll be there soon. Abigail is coming up first with the food. By subway. She should be there any sec."

"Just her? Yippee."

"Look, Gilly, grow up. She really went out of her way. She thought the two of you could get dinner ready together and set the table and stuff and then we'll all have a nice family meal for our first evening."

"I understand, Jeff, but ..."

"No buts. You promised." And he hangs up, the phone slamming in my ear.

I slam the phone too. Unfortunately, in nobody's ear.

What am I going to do?

I have to go.

I could tell Airhead that I'm having a fight with my best friend so I made other plans for tonight.

But I don't want to do that. She'll think, "The girl can't even get along with kids ... no wonder I have trouble."

Maybe I'll just leave a note saying that I had to go but that I'd love to make breakfast for them tomorrow.

That's what I'll do.

I better get dressed and get out of here before I have to face her.

I better ...

The doorbell.

Uh oh.

I don't want to see Airhead.
I don't want her in my house. In my home.
The bell rings again.
Don't panic, Gilly. The new Gilly doesn't panic.
So what am I going to do?
I run to my room and slam the door.

Chapter 21

*T*he doorbell rings again.

I have to answer it. She knows I'm here.

On the other hand . . . maybe I could get dressed and sneak down the fire escape.

On the other hand, we have no fire escape.

Rrring.

Okay already, Airhead. Okay. Don't be pushy.

I walk down the hall and open our door.

There she is. In tight jeans, carrying light-gray parachute baggage and a large shopping bag.

Her earrings are diamond strings and they glitter.

Even when she's packing and moving, even when all other human beings would be a mess, she's still gorgeous.

"Can I come in?" she says, and smiles.

"Uh . . . yeah. Sure."

"For a second I thought you weren't home or . . . wouldn't answer the door or something." She laughs.

"Hahaha," I laugh back. "Uh . . . can I help you with those?"

I try to calm down.

"Sure. Here, take this." And she shoves the shopping bag toward my chest.

As she follows me into the apartment, I chat to relax myself.

"Jeff just called," I say. "I didn't uh . . . I uh . . . wasn't expecting you so late."

Airhead looks at her watch. "I know." She smiles. "The boys are going to be stuck in traffic too, so I thought we'd make dinner. It's all in that bag."

"Right."

"But first . . . I've got to go to the little girls' room. Is it down here?"

I point down the hall.

Did she say "the little girls' room"?

Someone get me an emergency barf bag.

She is standing in front of a door which she thinks is the john. It's the linen closet.

I should just let her walk in. But I can't.

"Uh, Abigail, it's the next door down. That's the linen closet."

Abigail laughs another tinkly little laugh. "Thanks." And she wiggles into the john.

I look at my watch.

Maybe I'll offer her a cup of coffee. And then tell her I have to go.

Walking into the kitchen, I take the teakettle from

the back burner and fill it with water. Every second of chatting is going to make me later, and risk running into Doris . . . or Shep . . . or Don Melnick. Or somebody I don't want to see.

I hear the flush of the toilet, and then Abigail walks down the hall, passes the kitchen, looks around a little, and comes back.

"This is very lovely," she says. She picks up a little wooden puzzle on the coffee table.

"Very nice . . ."

"Thanks. We got it a few years ago when the whole family went to the Cape on a vacation."

She drops it like a hot potato.

"Uh, Abigail . . . you want some coffee?" I smile to take her mind off the sculpture.

"Sure . . . that would be great. By the way, Gilly. Your Dad and I . . . we'll be staying in the den . . . okay?"

They're not going to stay in my parents' bedroom. Hmm. That's very considerate of them.

She follows me into the kitchen.

"So . . ." she starts again, "in about twenty minutes we'll start dinner. Okay?"

"Uh . . . well . . . Abigail . . . this is the thing . . ."

She isn't listening. She puts the shopping bag on the kitchen table and starts taking out cartons of food as she talks.

"I went to Manzini's and got us a special Italian meal. Antipasto. Chicken cacciatore. We'll make the risotto."

She's really trying. But what can I do?

I don't want to be the bad guy.

But I just can't stay.

"Uh . . . Abigail. There's a tiny problem. See . . . I won't be here for dinner. I wanted to be, but there's been a misunderstanding. I have to be downtown by seven thirty. And I thought we would have eaten at five . . . that's when we usually eat. And . . . and now . . ." I look at my watch. "I have to get dressed practically this second."

She stares at me. "You're kidding . . ." Then she stares at all the food she's just put on the table.

I shake my head.

"I see." Her voice freezes up a bit. "In other words, if I hadn't come up early, you wouldn't have even been here."

"Well, I'm shooting this movie with a friend and . . ."

She picks up a bottle of soda and puts it in the refrigerator. She shuts the door with a slam.

"Your mother said you promised to have dinner with us first."

"I'm sorry, Abigail. I . . . maybe I planned too many things tonight. But I can't stay. I just can't."

She says nothing, just keeps staring at me.

I look down. "I mean, if you'd told me that you wanted me to hang out here till eight, eight thirty, I would have told my friends. But nobody told me."

"I see." Now she turns away. "There does appear to be a misunderstanding, doesn't there." And then she pivots back and looks me in the eye. "Or perhaps . . . perhaps you planned it badly . . . accidentally on purpose . . . hmmm, Gilly?"

Great. The psychoanalysis number. Fabulous.

"It wasn't on purpose, Abigail. It wasn't . . . I . . . I just have to go. I have to get dressed right now."

"Fine. Go ahead. That's great."

"I could still make the coffee."

"Don't bother."

"The Chock Full o' Nuts is in the fridge."

"I'll find it! I'll find it! Just go!"

I back out the door. "Really . . . I . . . I'm sorry. I love chicken cacciatore. That was very very thoughtful of you. Really . . ."

She turns around and ignores me. And mutters, "What's the use of trying." She mutters to herself, but she knows I hear her.

Damn her. I stayed an extra twenty minutes to talk. I risked running into everybody just to be nice and what do I get? I start to walk toward my room, but then I turn around.

"Yeah, Airhead. What's the use of either of us trying? It's a waste of time!" I shout. "So don't bother anymore. And I won't either."

I slam the door shut.

Chapter 22

Just when I thought I was getting a handle on things . . .
The handle comes off in my hand.

I'm sitting on the subway trying to calm down.

I take a deep breath.

I have to forget it.

It's so confusing.

Abigail was nice. She was. For over five minutes.

But then she lost her temper again.

Anyway, what's she so mad at? I mean, what did she do that was so great? Order take-out food? And what does it mean to bring chicken cacciatore and be nice for a few minutes when you've stolen another woman's husband?

Maybe I did know I'd have no time. But so what.

I'll tell you so what.

It's giving me an upset stomach. That's what.

I have to forget about it.

Forget that I have a stranger living in my apartment, sleeping in my mother's house with my father.

Forget I have a brother who was born without the gene for sensitivity.

Forget that my oldest friend ought to appear on a game show and answer questions on her new specialty —famous sadists.

I have to forget all this because it's not important.

It's time to make the movie.

It's going to be fun. Just like the other day.

I loved acting the other day. It made me feel so much better about everything.

I close my eyes and picture myself old and gnarled and wrinkled. I feel old. I am old. I can do it.

I'll be like Mrs. Hearn, my old neighbor.

Sweet, kind Mrs. Hearn. She'll be my model.

One more subway stop.

I open my eyes and look around the subway car. Graffiti. Dirt. Newspapers on the floor. Typical subway stuff.

Oh, yuk. A total creep is looking at me from the other end of the car. He's got to be older than my father, and he's smiling at me. He has a stubbly beard and hair so long it looks like a wig.

I look down at the dirty floor.

This is the part I hate about New York. Weirdos.

Oh, my God. He's walking toward me.

He's walking toward me!

Please, God. Pullease . . . don't start with me tonight.

He's getting closer. Closer.

He's right in front of me.

He winks. "Hiya . . ." he says. "Don't you look pretty . . ."

He starts to put his hand out toward me.

I lean back in my seat.

The car lurches. He lurches toward me.

I stand up, push him back, and I step on his toe with all my might.

"*Ayyyyyy!*" I hear him scream as I run for the subway doors.

"Gilly," I hear him shout. "Wait for me!"

Did he say Gilly? Uh oh.

I turn around.

The weirdo obviously knows me.

He pulls at his hair and it comes off.

"Hi . . . it's Mr. Norton . . . Victory's dad. I'm so sorry." He is laughing. "I forgot what I looked like. I'm going downtown to be in the movie, too!"

Sure enough, as I look more closely, I see that's who it is. The stubble on his cheek is painted on.

Now I smile. He walks toward me and we both walk out of the station together.

"I just didn't think," he says as we climb the subway stairs, coming out on Astor Place. "I started to daydream and then I saw you and I just forgot that I looked like a derelict." Now he grins. He has dimples.

"See, Victory wants me to play her father as a street person. You know Victory. She says her ultimate fear is that since I'm a painter I'll be so poor that I'll wind up on the street."

"Gee . . ."

"It would never happen, of course. But she wants to film me this way . . . and then in a smoking jacket in front of the Metropolitan Museum of Art. I'll tell you, being Victory's dad is . . . well . . . an adventure." He grins again.

I look at him, impressed. "It sure takes courage to ride in the subway like that, Mr. Norton."

"I know it. But when Victory told me what you were going to do, I thought that was pretty terrific too."

"Me?"

"You know . . . she's putting you in the beard and the long white robe. . . ."

"Yeah. I know."

"And you have to rattle a tambourine and chant in front of the Greenwich movie theater . . . and then make a raving speech trying to take converts. That takes guts!"

"What? You must have it wrong."

I'm shaking my head at him as I see Victory and Arnold out of the corner of my eye. They're waving their hands over their heads, wild with friendliness.

I don't wave back.

He must be wrong. He must be. I'm not playing a lunatic on a public street. Victory wouldn't do that to me.

I stare as they approach us. Arnold is wearing a black Stones T-shirt and sunglasses. He's holding Victory's hand, probably because he can't see in the dark with the shades.

"Yo!" he shouts at me. "Is that you, Gil?"

It can't be.

These are my best friends. As of last week.

I mean, if you can't trust your new best friends, who can you trust?

Victory waves to me again. In her hand is a tambourine.

Chapter 23

*W*here were you guys?" *Victory cries as she comes* up to us, embracing her father and then me. She kisses me on the cheek, and I am turning away as she begins to kiss me on the other cheek. This causes her to miss and kiss my scarf.

She takes a little wool fuzz out of her mouth as she speaks. "Dad, you look great," she says, and then looks at me. "And you look miserable, Gil."

I shrug.

"I just left Airhead and we had a welcome talk that turned into a goodbye talk."

"Did you tell her off?"

"No. Not exactly. I just told her I had to leave and she got mad at me. And . . . I got a little mad myself."

"Good! Look, you did what you had to do. You can't

be swayed by one demand, then another demand. You promised us you'd be in the movie."

"Right!"

She tosses my costume to me.

"Uh, wait a second, Victory," I say. "What's this about chanting and raving. You're kidding, right?"

She shakes her head. "Nope. I told you this would be more of a challenge. I see myself as an old wise woman, but still a little crazy. I don't know what I'll believe in then, but I'll still believe in something. So I want you to improvise . . . just be old . . . and shake the tambourine a little . . . and talk to yourself . . . and talk to strangers. We won't hear what you say because it's silent anyway . . . but just let go . . . be a little crazy. Get the idea?"

"Uh . . . yeah. But . . . that's not so easy."

"No . . . especially for you . . . but . . . it'll be fun. Here . . . put on this sandwich board, too. This might help you get in the mood." She hands me two signs attached by string. I read them before I put them over my head.

The one I wear in front says FREEDOM NOW. The one in back says EAT SUNFLOWER SEEDS.

I smile.

"Okay . . . are you ready, Gil? We'll start with a little exercise to make you feel old and crazy and loose. Like you are too old to care what anybody thinks. . . ."

"Yeah. Good idea. An exercise to make me not care what anybody thinks." I pull my beard into place. I feel like a total jerk. But I'm going to try. "What should I do?"

"You know that old song, 'You Can't Always Get

What You Want'? Take the tambourine and bang it, and skip down the street, singing it. Okay?"

"Whoa. That's the exercise? Victory . . . that's worse than the movie . . . It's so . . . so . . ."

"So crazy and uninhibited and wonderful and brilliant?"

"No . . . so crazy and uninhibited and stupid and dopey!"

Victory shakes her head. "All right. I can't make you, Gilly. I'll do it. Forget it."

"Sorry. Maybe I'm not in a crazy mood tonight."

"Like you usually are, you mean." Arnold snorts with laughter. Victory shakes her head.

Arnold comes up to me. "You are really something. She's depending on you. What's the matter with you, Gilly? You aren't even giving it a try."

"But, Arnold. You know me. I mean . . . I'm shy. I can't do that. I just can't. Even if my head said yes, my body would go into shy arrest. It wouldn't move. Believe me, Arnold. I know my body. We live together. It won't go along with it."

Arnold nods. "But I thought you were trying to change."

"I am, I am. But this is major surgery. It's so much so soon . . . don't you think?"

He shakes his head and I stroke my beard.

"All right. I'll try."

"Great! Look, you're not going to get over your shyness just thinking about it. If you want to be outrageous, you have to act outrageous."

I nod.

"It's just that . . . I think I'd rather act outrageous

121

doing what I want to do . . . you know? I feel every-body's always telling me what to do. And to them it's perfectly normal : . . but to me, it's nuts."

"What do you mean?"

"I mean, to my parents it's perfectly normal to live with a twenty-eight-year-old bubble bath model, and if I don't want to, that's not being nice. You know?"

Arnold nods.

"And to Victory it's perfectly normal to act like a wackadoo and run down Sixth Street in a beard but . . . am I crazy or is *that* crazy?"

"It's for your own good, Gil. If you want to get over your shyness."

"I know . . . I know."

He takes off the sunglasses and looks around.

"Hmmm . . . nice night," he says, and then, "Look, don't you think I'm nervous? I have to be the camera-man tonight and I've never done it."

"Yeah . . . that's scary."

"And then tomorrow . . . I'm actually going to be in the movie and I'm really scared. I mean . . . I have to shoot a sex scene . . . seminude. Just my gym shorts."

"Really? Wow. That takes guts too!"

"You're damn right!"

"Well . . . if you can do that . . . I mean, that's pretty good . . ."

I'm talking, but my brain, like a VCR, is rewinding and then slowly playing back what Arnold just said.

It couldn't be.

I mean—she would have told me.

It just couldn't be.

I better ask.

"Uh, Arnold . . . this nude scene . . . who . . . uh . . . who's playing Victory?"

He doesn't move a muscle in his mouth as the word comes out: "You."

Of course.

Even Arnold looks scared as I make this incredible face. Scrunching up my nose. Turning my hands into fists. Widening my eyes. Clamping down my teeth so I look like an angry halloween mask.

I scream. At the top of my lungs.

"Neverrrrrrr!"

Then I turn and run. My eyes are still wide, my legs are moving under me and I am running for the subway.

Past people, past stores, past cars, down the subway steps, where I put my token in the turnstile, where a car is waiting, and where before I know it, I've ditched my beard and sandwich boards and am heading uptown.

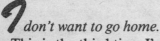
Chapter 24

I don't want to go home.

This is the third time I'm walking from the subway stop at 86th and Broadway up to 96th and Broadway.

I don't know what to do.

I'm so upset. I just keep walking.

It's as though all the feelings are in my legs, and my brain is numb.

Every once in a while I come to my senses and realize what I've done.

I calmly think: "Hmm—I ran away and behaved like a total idiot."

"Hmm—I ruined Victory's movie. And I've ruined my life."

But then I walk some more, and look in shop windows and think, "Hmmm . . . interesting. They have a sale on jeans."

I have to talk to somebody.

Unfortunately, though, at the moment, everybody I need to talk to—I'm no longer talking to.

I spot a phone booth.

I hate to do this to her. I hate to—but I have to.

Reaching the booth, I deposit a quarter as I rummage through my knapsack, find my wallet, and pull out the piece of paper with my mom's phone number.

I dial, and the operator asks for more money. I rummage again. One quarter. Two quarters. A piña colada Lifesaver. Another quarter. Finally I find enough, and my Uncle Billy's phone starts to ring.

"Hello?" A deep voice answers the phone.

"Uncle Billy? This is Gilly. Is my mom there?"

"Gilly? Sure! She's right here. We just walked in from the airport. Did you call to make sure she was all right?"

"Uh . . . yeah."

I hear him explaining, and then my mom gets on the phone.

"Hi, Gil! Everything okay?"

"No!"

"What's the matter?"

"Everything. Everything is rotten. The house is rotten. The movie is rotten. My friends are rotten . . . my life is rotten." Then, just so she doesn't get hysterical long distance, I add, "So . . . how was your flight?"

"My flight was fine. Talk to me, Gil. What happened?"

"I told you. Everything. I had a fight with Airhead. And . . . and I ran away from making the movie. And I don't have any friends. And I don't have any family. And . . ."

Since I'm standing on the corner of 90th Street, I try not to cry.

But then my mom says, in a soothing sympathetic, loving, mommy voice, "Awww . . . honey . . . love . . ." And tears start to flow.

"Mommee . . ." I moan, "can I come to California? Please. Please."

I know I sound like a three-year-old, but I can't help it.

"Gilly . . . come on now . . . calm down."

Just then a recorded voice says, "I'm sorry . . . your three minutes are up. Please deposit ninety cents."

I'm sobbing now, in jerks and heaves, so hard that I can't speak.

"Oh, Gilly. Please . . . just calm down . . ."

"Huh . . . huh . . . huh . . ." I cry.

"Listen, I'll call you back. Just . . . tell me the number on the pay phone and I'll call you right back. Right right back."

I look at the phone. The number is scratched off.

I can't believe it.

"Huh . . . there's huh . . . no number, Ma."

"Okay, don't panic, Gil. Just let me think. Look, you call me back collect, okay? And we'll talk about what you should do next. Okay?"

"Okay." I turn around. People are looking at me.

So I hang up. And I start to walk again.

I try to wipe away my tears without being obvious.

I try to calm down.

My mom's going to worry about me if I don't call her back.

That's not nice. Calling her and then leaving her hanging like that.

Like having a kid and then . . . walking out.

I mean I don't hate my mom. She's nice.

Even my dad's nice. It's not his fault he fell in love with an Airhead.

Even Airhead tried to be nice tonight. For five minutes anyway.

I hate adults.

And I'm not too crazy about kids either.

Other people can be so disappointing.

On the other hand, it doesn't seem so healthy of me to be angry at every human being I know. Maybe there's something wrong with me, too.

Nah.

None of this is my fault. None of it.

What's my fault is that I take it. That I want it. That I would put an ad in the paper to get it.

But no more.

No more Miss Nice Girl.

I'm angry.

Yes, I am. I'm ticked off.

I've had it. I don't want to live with a twenty-eight-year-old Barbie doll. I don't want to have to drop one friend because another friend doesn't like it. I don't want to dance down the street in a beard in the movie of someone else's life.

This is my life!

I'm going to do what *I* want to do.

If only I knew what it was. . . .

But I do know what it is.

At least it's the only thing I can think of.

I walk to the corner of 90th Street, but this time I don't cross. Instead I look both ways and utter the one word necessary to take me to freedom.

"Taxi!"

Chapter 25

I am standing outside the Florence Nightingale Senior Citizens' Hotel.

It's only ten o'clock. That's not bad.

Mrs. Hearn should still be up.

I'm nervous, but I push the revolving doors and enter.

The lobby is an enormous old room, with walls of dark wood. It's filled with chairs that are filled with grandma-type faces. The chairs are lined against the wall, and all the faces seem to look up when the door opens. I swallow nervously and walk to the desk. I peek around. Whoever I look at smiles at me.

"I'd like to see Mrs. Hearn, please. Mrs. Gladys Hearn."

"Is she expecting you?" the man says.

"Uh huh."

"She's in the TV room. Down the corridor."

"Thanks."

I walk until I reach a room with a glass door. I peek in and sure enough, there's a TV. And there's Mrs. Hearn, sitting on a chair, her eyes closed. A couple of other women are watching the set.

I tiptoe in and walk over to her.

"Mrs. Hearn?" I say, shaking her shoulder a tiny bit.

She starts and then opens her eyes.

"Mrs. Hearn. It's me. Gilly."

She squints.

God, I hope since I last saw her she's not senile or anything.

"Gilly? Is that you?" She squints again.

She can't see so well. I remember my mom saying that her eyes were getting worse.

"Yes . . . It is. It's Gilly."

She shakes her head, reaching for something on the table beside her.

"If you're looking for your glasses, maybe they're in your pocket. You always used to keep them in your housecoat."

She reaches into her pocket and sure enough, there they are. Putting them on, she looks at me.

"Gilly! What are you doing here? Did you forget your keys again?"

I shake my head. "Uh uh. I came because . . . because I wanted to talk to you." I look around. Three old ladies are staring at me. "Can we talk alone?"

"Sure. Of course. We'll go up to my apartment. Come."

I realize old people are nice and everything. And they're lonely. But if I don't know them, they make me nervous.

Mrs. Hearn struggles out of her chair.

"I don't know why they call these chairs easy chairs. They aren't." She grins. "Follow me."

We walk down the hall toward the back of the hotel. When we get to Apartment 1G she takes out her key, fiddles with the lock, and lets us into her apartment.

"Come in. Make yourself at home."

I do. And I look around. There's the big old mahogany breakfront I used to see almost every day. And the coffee table with all the drawers. And her velvet couch. And her doilies. And her books. They all look a little out of place, like they don't really belong here, but it's good to see them.

When she closes the door and turns around, she takes a long look at me.

She gives me a big hug and kiss and I hold her tight.

"So?" she says.

"So . . . so I missed you."

"I missed you too."

"I'm sorry I didn't call or anything."

"That's okay. I've been keeping track." She walks toward a little kitchenette and I follow. "In fact, your mom called me last week . . . you have such a nice mom."

"No, I don't! She left. She moved to California. I'm all alone!"

Mrs. Hearn's eyes widen. "She left you all alone? No!"

"Well . . . not exactly. She left me with . . . strangers!"

"Strangers?"

"Well, not exactly. She left me with my father. And . . . his girlfriend! They moved in today."

"Tsk tsk tsk." Mrs. Hearn shakes her head.

"So . . . I was thinking . . . Maybe you want some company . . ."

"Company?"

"This seems like a very good place for me to live. It's got hundreds of grandmothers. I think I'd like it here." I walk over to the velvet couch and touch the back of it gently.

"But, Gilly . . . this is not your home. It's not even my home. It's . . . a hotel. Nobody should live here."

"But we could keep each other company. I could help you find your glasses. Stuff like that."

"Ah-ha."

"See, Mrs. Hearn, I thought it through. I could take the crosstown bus to school every day. And then I'd come back here every night. What do you say? Can I stay?"

She looks at me and then around the room. "I . . . don't know." She goes to the refrigerator. "Why don't we talk a little. And have some tuna fish. You hungry?"

I nod. "I'm starved. I . . . uh . . . skipped dinner."

"You set the table, the silverware is in that drawer. And I'll put up the tea and tuna. Okay?"

"Okay."

I get out her familiar old forks and knives and napkins and start to set the little Formica table.

I could be happy here. I could.

Mrs. Hearn is like my family.

I look up and watch as she smashes the tuna fish with a fork.

Her tuna fish is totally different than the kind my mom makes with the food processor. It's lumpier.

In Mrs. Hearn's day, everything was different. From the furniture to the tuna fish.

Finally, we sit.

Mrs. Hearn takes a cracker and pushes some tuna fish onto it. Then she hands it to me. "You know, Gilly, when I moved here I was very unhappy. So unhappy. My daughter. My son. They felt terrible that they had to put me here. They said, 'What can we do?' and then they did it."

"Believe me, I understand. That's terrible."

"I was very angry."

"Me, too. That's how I feel. Very angry."

She passes me another cracker and then goes on. "Even though there was nothing they could do. They didn't have room for me. I do need medical care. It's nobody's fault exactly . . . but I'm still angry. Is that how you feel?"

I shake my head. "Kind of. But it is somebody's fault. My parents shouldn't have gotten divorced. Period."

"You want to know something, Gilly? And this is between you and me. I was married forty-six years. And every day I thought, 'Who needs this?' I didn't leave but . . . I wanted to. I didn't leave because of my son and daughter." She looks around the room. "I think I was stupid. I did that for my children and my children put me here. I'll tell you the truth. Children today . . ." She hits the air with the palm of her hand, like she's saying, "Who needs them?"

I nod in agreement. "Parents today . . ." And I flick my wrist too.

We smile.

"Look, Gil, the main thing is that you build your own life. You have friends your own age . . . like Franny . . ."

"I, uh . . ." I shake my head. "Friends today . . ."

"What do you mean? What happened between you and Franny?"

I shrug. "We're not talking." And I swat the air with my hand.

Mrs. Hearn nods. "Did you ever meet my friend Agnes? The one who taught biology at the same high school where I taught math? She was my best friend. But she was a gossip. We didn't speak for three years."

"Really? What did she do?"

"I don't remember. I remember she was wrong and I was right. That's for sure. But, three years. I missed her. You should stay friends with Franny."

"She threw a big party tonight and invited everybody. Everybody but me, Mrs. Hearn!"

Mrs. Hearn shakes her head. So do I.

And together we both say, "People today . . ."

And we start to laugh. And laugh.

"I don't want to go home, Mrs. Hearn. I just don't want to! Please. Please don't make me!"

She peers at me over her reading glasses.

"Please . . ."

"Tsk tsk tsk," she says. And then she gets up.

"We should call your father," she says. "I'll call him."

134

"And . . . and my mom. I . . . uh . . . hung up on her on Broadway. She might be . . . uh . . . a little hysterical."

Mrs. Hearn nods. "I'll talk to them. I'll . . . I'll tell them that you're going to stay here . . . at least till tomorrow. Okay?"

"Yeah! Yeah!"

And I grin so hard I can feel it in my ears.

<u>Chapter 26</u>

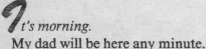*t's morning.*

My dad will be here any minute.

He thinks he's coming to pick me up.

But I'm not going.

Last night, Mrs. Hearn and I stayed up until one o'clock. We just kept talking and talking.

And we're still talking over cornflakes and bananas.

Now she peers at me over her glasses. "You know, Gilly, when I first moved to this hotel, I felt it was so hopeless that . . . I considered . . . suicide."

"Really? Oh, gee. Oh. That's . . . that's terrible."

I pause and look at her. "You know," I begin, trying to be as honest as she is, "I understand how you felt because . . . because when my parents got divorced, it crossed my mind too."

She nods.

I can't believe I admitted that. But it's true.

"I mean like it ran across my mind . . . and left," I say. "Anyway, it would be very messy. I didn't really want to."

"I understand," she says. "I didn't really want to either. So how are you feeling now?"

"Well, now I just feel crazy. I want to be happy. I want to be myself. I don't want what everyone else wants for me anymore . . . I want to decide."

"That's good, Gilly. That's very good."

"It is? Then why does it feel so terrible?"

Mrs. Hearn smiles.

"What is it that you do want?"

"Well, for starters, I want my mom back . . . and I'd like to be friends with Franny and Victory and even Arnold again. And not have to choose between them."

"That sounds reasonable. Is that all?"

"Well, I . . . I want to feel more confident . . . And . . . and I'd like a boyfriend. And I'd like to get into the Bronx High School of Science. And I'd like people to take me seriously. And I'd like to have more courage. And I'd like to be more adventurous. And . . . is that too much to ask?"

"Much too much."

I nod. "I know . . . but it doesn't have to come all at once. Just a little bit every day."

"I guess it doesn't help if I tell you that by the time you're grown up you'll probably have all of it."

"No. Because I don't have confidence now. I don't like things the way they are right now! That's why . . . I'd rather live here. At least . . . I want to . . ."

"I understand. Your dad will be very upset. But I understand."

She gets up from her chair and turns on her television.

Kids and old people have a lot in common.

We both watch a lot of television.

She turns the dial until she hits a rerun of *Leave It to Beaver*.

"I love that show," I say. "Can we watch it?"

"Sure," she says.

Great.

I'm crazy about the Cleavers.

Whatever Beaver worries about, it gets better at the end of the half hour.

That's so . . . so relaxing.

I wonder what Beaver would decide if he were in my shoes.

Would he rather live in an old-age home or would he rather live with Ward and his teenage girlfriend?

The phone rings. Mrs. Hearn picks it up and listens.

"That was the desk, Gilly," she says, hanging up and arching her eyebrows. "Your dad's on his way up."

Chapter 27

Gilly, do you think you're being fair?" My father stands in Mrs. Hearn's living room.

He looks terrible.

"I mean, you haven't even given Abigail a chance. I don't want to have to force you to come home. I know how unhappy you are. But it was hard for us to move to West End, too. We did it for you."

He's wearing a gray corduroy shirt and a pink tie. Airhead obviously dressed him this morning.

"Dad, you can't force me back . . . because I won't go!"

"Then what do you want me to do?"

"I don't know." I stare at the television.

"Gilly, please turn the TV off."

The phone rings, and Mrs. Hearn picks it up.

"It's for you, Gilly."

I get up and take the receiver as my father turns off the television.

"Hello?"

"Hello? Gilly? It's me. Are you okay?"

It's Arnold. "Hi . . ." I say.

"Gilly, I just wanted to tell you that uh . . . Victory took your part in the movie last night. After all, when you wear a robe and beard, nobody can tell who it is anyway. Right?"

"I suppose so."

"So . . . it was no big deal. So . . . how's Mrs. Hearn? Pretty old, huh?"

"She's fine."

"When are you coming home?"

"Why, Arnold? Do you have math homework for tomorrow?"

"No . . . It's just that we want to talk. And Franny wants to talk. And you know . . . we're all . . . you know . . . like my mother would say . . . concerned about you."

My whole world now knows what I've done. I've really made a scene.

"I don't know, Arnold . . ."

"Franny's right here. And so is Victory. You want to talk to either of them?"

"What? What are Franny and Victory doing in the same room?"

"Well . . . there was a special handwritten edition of *West End Avenue Winds* this morning which mentioned you're . . . uh . . . leaving. Uh . . . so the three of us got together. Do you want to talk to them or not?"

140

"No. Not now," I say as coldly as I can.

"Gilly, we miss you. We really do."

"That's nice. Can I call you later? My father's here."

"Uh . . . just a sec." I hear his voice, muffled, saying, "She wants to call us later," and then he gets back on the phone. "Sure."

"Okay. 'Bye, Arnold."

"Uh, Gil. Just one more thing. I'm really sorry. I know it was all my fault . . ."

"Huh?"

"It was all my fault. I mean, the thought of doing a love scene with me is what made you run away from home, right?"

I laugh. "Arnold . . . it wasn't that . . . it was just that everybody's always telling me what to do."

"Oh. Is that all? Well, then . . . speak up. Tell us what you want! I'll listen to anybody. That's one of my best qualities."

I laugh again.

"Just a sec."

I hear him say, "She laughed." Then he gets back on the phone. "Franny wants to talk to you."

Before I can say no, she gets on.

"Gilly?"

"Hi, Fran. How are you?"

"I'm okay. Uh . . . I'm sorry I didn't invite you to the party."

"You should be."

There's silence on the phone.

Finally she speaks. "You weren't so nice either, you know."

I don't say anything at first. And then, "True."

"Well, I just thought you should know that I'm upset too. And . . . and if you'll say you're sorry, I will."

"I'm sorry!"

"I'm sorry!"

"Goodbye!"

"Goodbye!"

She hangs up. And so do I.

I turn back to my father.

I think I just made up with Franny.

It wasn't how I'd imagined it. I imagined her on her knees, groveling, but . . .

I feel a little better.

I walk back to my father.

He fidgets with his pink tie. "Look, Gilly. I know you're having trouble these days. But you have to accept Abigail. There's nothing else you can do. I care about her . . . and about you. And I care about your mother too."

"You're a very caring person. I'm going to nominate you for the Nobel Peace Prize."

"Don't be fresh!"

I turn away.

Mrs. Hearn walks over to me and puts her arm around me.

"Gilly," she says, "you know I enjoyed your visit. I really did. And I'd love you to visit again. I could use the company . . . but . . ."

"Mrs. Hearn! You promised!"

"You could come Fridays sometimes. That would be

nice. You know I'm not well. I don't know if I could handle a teenager full-time anymore."

Mrs. Hearn shakes her head as my father walks toward me.

I have to say what I think.

I don't want to go home. Not with him. And her.

He keeps walking toward me, his arms out.

I back up.

I have to say what I think.

"Don't you understand, Dad!" I scream. "Don't you understand how much you've hurt us. Me. Mom. You've done a terrible thing. And I can't forgive you. I'll never forgive you. Never!"

He steps back as though he was hit.

I've said it. I've thought it so many times. But I've finally said it.

He just stares at me, shaking his head.

It takes a long time until he says, "Gilly, I'm sorry, very sorry that you feel that way. But I'm your father. You're my responsibility for the next three months. I won't disappear."

I don't say anything.

"Gilly, remember when you told me about Jessica Parrington? That her dad moved to Paris and started a new family? And she's never seen him since? Remember, you said, 'How can a father do that?' Well, I won't do that. I just won't . . ."

He's standing right in front of me now.

"Gilly, you're my daughter. I love you. And I know you love me, no matter how angry you are."

"Dad," I scream. "That's the point . . . that's the point!"

"Huh?"

My back is against the living room wall.

I shake my head and lower my voice. "Don't you see, Dad? In our house it's just so easy to say I love you. It always has been. 'I wish I had more time for you, Gilly, I love you.' 'We're getting divorced I love you.' 'I have a girlfriend and I'm moving in with her I love you.'" I look at him. He doesn't get it. "Don't you understand, Dad? You left. You walked out. Right now . . . what hurts . . . what hurts so much"—I try not to look at his eyes—"is that I don't love you."

My eyes fill with tears and I shake my head. "I don't love you. . . ." And I start to sob.

I look at him. His eyes are filling with tears too.

How could I say something so horrible?

But it's what I feel.

I can't just love him no matter what. Jeff can. Jeff's a forgiver. But I can't.

"I'm sorry, Dad. I want to love you. I swear I do. But . . . I can't." I shake my head.

Mrs. Hearn walks over to me and puts her hands on my shoulders.

"You know, Gilly . . . it wasn't just your dad who wanted the divorce. Your mom did too."

"I know. I know." But I don't really believe it.

"Your dad never wanted to say anything bad about your mom, but . . . they were both unhappy. I know. I talked to her a lot."

I shrug.

She puts an arm around me.

"Tell me, Gilly, do you remember when you *did* love your dad?"

I wipe away a tear. I don't say anything.

"C'mon, Gil. Try to remember . . . for me," she says.

I take a deep breath. "I loved him when he lived with us . . ."

"Uh huh . . ."

"I . . . I loved him when we spent time together. When we played Scrabble together all night. I loved him when we took long walks on Broadway and talked . . . and talked. I loved him when he loved me. And . . . showed it."

Uh oh. I'm crying again.

My father walks over to me and puts his arms around me. And hugs me.

I love him now.

We just stand there for a minute, holding each other, my face in his shirt.

"I understand," he says. "I really do."

I nod. "It's so confusing, Dad. It's so hard to feel more than one thing. I do . . . I do love you and I . . . do hate you for what you did. And . . . maybe . . . maybe with both feelings inside me I just . . . I just love you less."

I know that hurts him again. But that's the truth.

He shakes his head but he doesn't move away. He holds me tight. And then bends a little until his eyes are level with mine.

He smiles. He strokes my hair.

"So . . . you love me . . . but you love me less . . ."

"Uh huh . . ."

He strokes my hair. "How much less . . ."

"I can't tell exactly right now . . . when you're hugging me."

And I can't help it. I grin.

I look at Mrs. Hearn. She's grinning too.

We all stand there for a second.

Then she puts an arm around both of us.

"Well, I'll tell you. I don't think love has anything to do with it. It's just been a lousy year."

We nod. I take a deep breath.

For the first time in a long time I feel different. I don't feel . . . so angry.

"Yeah, it has," she says. "But . . . uh . . . now . . . I've got to get downstairs. Mrs. Abernathy is eighty-seven today. Big party. Big big party. Just blowing out the candles will take the whole afternoon."

My dad and I both grin.

But now what do we do?

"Gilly, I want to call home now. Abigail was very upset. She really was."

"Dad, she got mad so fast . . . really, she did."

"Maybe. But she tried." He turns toward the phone.

"I'm going to call her. But I'm going to tell her that we've talked and that . . . we'd like to go away for a couple of days. Just the two of us. Maybe to the Cape. We haven't done that in a long time. A long long time."

He looks at me expectantly.

"What do you say, Gil?"

"I'd love to, Dad." I take a deep breath.

"But, then . . . then we have to go home. We all have to try again."

I nod.

Mrs. Hearn goes to the refrigerator and takes out a box of mints.

"You can eat them on the trip." She pauses. "Did I ever tell you I hated my mother-in-law, Gilly?"

I shake my head.

She nods. "I always had to be nice to her, but it was never easy. Never. The woman was a witch."

"Really?"

"Oh, yeah. When I first got married, she took me to Saks and made me buy the ugliest vanity. I'm talking ugly. But what was I going to do? I wanted to be respectful so I bought it. I saw that woman twice a month for thirty years. I had no choice. My husband loved her."

I sniffle and smile.

Now she looks at my dad. "Not that Abigail's a witch, Morty. But you understand . . . she just may not be Gilly's type. That's the way it is sometimes."

"I understand, Mrs. Hearn."

"I know you do. And I know Gilly will endure. Because she's very special. And I'm a good judge of that sort of thing."

I blush.

"I'll come visit real soon, Mrs. Hearn. I promise. Friday maybe. And thanks. Thanks a lot."

"You're welcome, Gilly."

I put on my coat.

When your hands are full of fruit and mints and cookies, it isn't easy, but Mrs. Hearn and I hug for as long as possible.

Chapter 28

*Y*ou can freeze your long underwear off on Cape Cod in March.

I'm still shivering in the car, looking for a parking space in New York.

We had a good time. We really did.

My dad rented a court at an indoor tennis center, so we played a couple of hours of tennis each day.

We took long, freezing walks on the dunes, too. And had lobster both nights.

We didn't talk that much to each other.

But that was okay.

And we called my mom both nights.

She said she was sorry that she had to go to California. But she didn't say she loved me in the same sentence.

My dad must have talked to her.

I told my mom I could last three months.

I'm going to try.

That must be why I'm shivering. I'm not cold. I'm scared.

As soon as we park, I have to go up there and meet Abigail alone again.

I'm even a little nervous about seeing Franny and Victory and Arnold again.

My dad spots a car pulling out of a space, and we park.

Walking to our building, he puts an arm around my shoulder.

"Ready?" he says.

"No. But let's go up."

We take the elevator to eleven. My dad takes his key out and when we get to the door he lets us in.

It's been a long time since he's done that.

"Abigail, we're home!" he says.

She comes out of the kitchen. She looks at me with a half smile, half nod. I do the same. My dad rushes over to her and gives her a kiss.

I force myself to watch.

I guess I have to get used to that stuff even though it's totally re-pulsivo.

"We brought dinner, Abigail," I say. "Four lobsters. Is Jeff here?"

"Not yet. He called though. He has some kind of after-school thing on Wednesdays. So . . . how was your trip?"

"Good. Really nice," my dad and I both say together.

I look closely at her. She's wearing a beautiful green sweater and tiny little silver cube earrings. Very chic.

I take a deep breath. "Uh . . . would you happen to know if Franny is home? I . . . I have to see her. I have to get all the work I missed at school."

"I'm sorry. I really don't know. But Victory called you. She asked you to call her immediately . . . she left this number." She gives me a piece of paper.

"Thanks." As I turn around to go to the phone, I see Abigail put her arms around my father's neck, and he stoops to kiss her.

She giggles and whispers, "How'd I do?"

I can't help it. I can't stand the woman.

I mean, she knows I'm still in the room.

She's such a baby, is what she is.

I don't like her voice.

And I'm definitely not crazy about her walk. When she walks, she wiggles slightly to the left.

Nope, I don't like her. I probably never will like her, just like Mrs. Hearn's mother-in-law.

But . . . I guess I can live with her.

I dial the number on the paper.

"Is Victory Norton there?"

"This is she. Gilly? Is that you?"

"Uh huh," I say. "Where are you?"

"I'm in Queens for the day. My school made us visit a career fair in Flushing today. So I'm sleeping over at my Aunt Florence's. It's kind of interesting, actually. Flushing. Uh . . . Gilly . . . you're not mad at me, are you?"

"No. Not really. I mean . . . are you mad at me? I'm sorry I ran away. I just couldn't handle it."

"I understand. But . . . uh . . . I scratched the sex

scene. On the other hand . . . how would you feel playing me as an infant? You know—coo coo. A little baby talk. A little fetal-position stuff. Huh?"

Oh, boy.

"Can I think about it before I say yes? Or think about how I could do it?"

"Hey, Gil . . . no problem."

"Good. I uh . . . I hear you and Franny sort of met."

"Yeah. She's not so bad. She might even help with the movie . . . be the stylist or something."

"Really?"

"Yeah. She's kind of okay. Like you said. So, see ya tomorrow." And she hangs up.

Hmm. Just what I wanted.

Victory and Franny to be friends . . .

Hmm. That's great.

All three of us will be friends.

Yeah. That's great.

Hmm.

I wonder if they talked about me.

I wonder if they like each other a whole lot.

I wonder if—I mean, they couldn't already . . . like each other more than they each like me.

Hold it! Stop worrying!

I refuse to worry!

At least . . . for the moment. Because I hear a door slam.

I'll bet that's Franny coming home from Barrow.

I take a deep breath, walk down the hall, past my dad and Abigail, who are sitting at the table having coffee.

"I'm going next door for a little while," I say casually.

"Okay, Gilly. See you soon," Abigail answers, kind of sweetly. I smile.

I let my door slam behind me and press Franny's doorbell.

The peephole opens and I see her green eyes.

"Hi!" she says, opening the door. "Come on in!"

She backs in, letting me lead the way to her room.

I plop down on her Indian bedspread.

"Hi!" I say nervously.

"Hi . . ." she says again.

"So . . . what's the story?" we say at practically the same time.

I tell her everything, from the movie to calling Victory.

Franny listens like only Franny can listen to me.

Then she says, "Well, I met Abigail while you were gone. She is definitely a robomatic. But she has incredible earrings! And she puts on makeup very well. In fact, there are a lot of things you could learn from her. And then you can teach them to your mom."

"Huh. You mean, so my mom can get my dad back?"

"No! So she can meet a movie star. Or a director. Or a rich Hollywood producer."

"Maybe. So . . . what about you? Were you wearing Don Melnick's class ring?"

"Uh . . . not exactly. It wasn't mine. It was this guy that Toby's seeing. From Bucknell. I just borrowed it because I wanted to see how it felt to wear a college ring around your neck. It felt great."

"How was the party?"

"Okay. A little weird. I think maybe I do like Don Melnick."

152

"Really?"

"I think so. I mean, not as much as Master X. But . . . I can't wait for Master X, you know what I'm saying. . . ."

"Absolutely. Did . . . uh . . . Shep wind up with anyone?"

"Uh uh. In fact, he asked a lot of questions about you."

"He did? Did he really?"

She nods a few times and moves to her night table.

"Sunday's another study group meeting, Gil."

"Yeah . . ." I say. "I think we better do some research. I . . . I missed that. A lot."

"Right. My thought exactly." And she opens her night-table drawer and takes out the deck of cards.

As she lays out the cards, she begins, "O great cards, O deck of destiny, O clubs and hearts . . . O spades and diamonds of infinite wisdom, we ask you today about the future of Gilly Miles, my oldest and my dearest—" She pauses. "My oldest and my dearest friend. . . ."

She looks up at me. And grins.

And so do I.

About the Author

SUSAN HAVEN has created material for Lily Tomlin's Edith Ann and for television shows such as "All in the Family." She has written two children's books and humorous pieces about children for *Redbook, Woman's Day, Ms., New York* and *The New York Times*. Ms. Haven lives with her husband and sixteen-year-old son in New York City. She is the author of *City Kids*, a Simon & Schuster Fireside book.